TALES FROM THE SCAREMASTER

VAMPIRE VACATION

D0051555

You don't have to read the

TALES FROM THE

SCAREMASTER

books in order. But if you want to,
here's the right order:

Swamp Scarefest

Werewolf Weekend

Clone Camp!

Zombie Apocalypse

Vampire Vacation

TALES FROM THE SCAREMASTER™

VAMPIRE VACATION

by B. A. Frade
and Stacia Deutsch

Little, Brown and Company
New York Boston

This book is a work of fiction. Names, characters, places, and incidents are the product of the author's imagination or are used fictitiously. Any resemblance to actual events, locales, or persons, living or dead, is coincidental.

Copyright © 2017 by Hachette Book Group, Inc.
Text written by Stacia Deutsch
Tales from the Scaremaster logo by David Coulson
TALES FROM THE SCAREMASTER and THESE SCARY STORIES WRITE
THEMSELVES are trademarks of Hachette Book Group

Cover design by Christina Quintero. Cover illustration by Scott Brundage.
Cover copyright © 2017 by Hachette Book Group, Inc.

Hachette Book Group supports the right to free expression and the value of copyright. The purpose of copyright is to encourage writers and artists to produce the creative works that enrich our culture.

The scanning, uploading, and distribution of this book without permission is a theft of the author's intellectual property. If you would like permission to use material from the book (other than for review purposes), please contact permissions@hbgusa.com. Thank you for your support of the author's rights.

Little, Brown and Company
Hachette Book Group
1290 Avenue of the Americas, New York, NY 10104
Visit us at lb-kids.com

First Edition: July 2017

Little, Brown and Company is a division of Hachette Book Group, Inc.
The Little, Brown name and logo are trademarks of Hachette Book Group, Inc.

The publisher is not responsible for websites (or their content) that are not owned by the publisher.

ISBNs: 978-0-316-46409-3 (pbk.), 978-0-316-4641-16 (ebook)

TALES FROM THE SCAREMASTER™

VAMPIRE VACATION

*Don't make the same mistake
Zoe and Matt made.
Don't read my book.*

—The Scaremaster

I warned you.

Chapter One

"What's in your bag, Matt?" I was smashed into a small sliver of seat in the third row of a rental van. I could barely move. "I'm squished here," I complained, shoving at the heavy duffel. It didn't budge. "This thing weighs a ton!"

The brown duffel was too big to fit in the trunk with the other luggage, so my dad had stuck it on the seat between Matt and me. After three hours of driving, with only one quick bathroom break, my legs were starting to cramp, and I was growing more and more crabby every minute.

"I was planning a surprise," Mateo Ortiz told me in a soft whisper only I could hear. "But if you *have* to know what's inside…" He gave me a sideways look with his dark brown eyes and waggled his eyebrows.

"Oh, good grief," I groaned. "Stop the dramatics. Tell me already!"

Matt paused another beat, then laughed. "Nah. I'm not telling."

"You're ridiculous." I rolled my eyes and tightened my blond ponytail. "I bet it's that new snowboard you got for your birthday. And maybe a basketball in case the lodge has an indoor court. And…" I considered what else he might have brought on vacation. "Your laptop so you don't miss any football games while we are away." Matt didn't just like one team. He liked them all.

Matt grinned and patted the duffel bag. "Maybe you're right…." He winked at me. "But maybe you're wrong."

"Stop acting like there's something amazing in this thing." I smacked my hand against it. Something lumpy poked me in the palm. "Ouch," I said, though it didn't really hurt.

"Ah, forget about it. You don't need to know." Matt plugged in his earbuds and leaned his head against the window.

I turned away from my best friend with a chuckle. This conversation wasn't over, and we both knew it.

"How much longer?" I asked my dad, who was navigating while Matt's dad drove.

"We'll be there soon," he replied, which had been his answer the last four times I'd asked.

With a sigh, I leaned forward. Maybe I could use the duffel as a pillow and rest awhile. "Ugh!" I immediately pulled back, adding, "Eww." I sat upright and poked Matt in the arm to get him to take out the earbuds. When he did, I said, "This mystery's solved. It smells like a dead body's in there."

"Way to go, Detective Lancaster. You're right!" He put up his hand for a high five. I ignored him, and he lowered it. "I know how much you like to be scared, Zo, so I thought we could create our own Frankenstein's monster." He placed a hand on the bag. "I brought everything we need: electrodes, wires, artificial heart, a fresh body...." Matt began to chuckle in a low, creepy voice. "We can get started tomorrow, right after we hit the slopes, of course."

"Mom!" Chloe whined from her comfortable seat in the middle row. She had plenty of room between Matt's mom and ours. "Zoe and Matt have a dead man stuffed in their bag." Chloe was eight years old and had amazing hearing. I had no doubt that my sister would be an excellent spy when she grew up. But that would only happen if she could learn to keep a secret.

The instant that Chloe got involved, the rules of the "What's in the duffel?" game changed. I was on Matt's side now.

"How do you know it's a man?" I teased her, winking at Matt before adding, "All you know is that it's a body."

Matt caught on immediately. "True," he whispered, quiet enough so Chloe could hear but our moms, who were busy chatting, couldn't. "It might be a dead woman...."

The terrified look on my sister's face was almost pathetic enough to make me feel bad about teasing her. That is, until she yelled, "MOM! Zoe and Matt are trying to scare me!"

"Cut it out, you two." My mom turned around to look at me and Matt. "Zoe Hannah Lancaster, you know better." Uh-oh. I knew I was in trouble when Mom used my whole name. "The ride's long enough without you torturing Chloe." She put a hand on Chloe's shoulder. "They're just joking around, sweetie," she said. "You know how the two of them are when they're together."

Matt and I had been friends before we were born. Seriously. Our dads were roommates in college, and our moms were pregnant at the same time. We were born just a few weeks apart twelve and a half years ago.

We didn't live in the same city but saw each other twice a year when our families vacationed together. Usually we'd go to a rented beach house, but this time our parental units jointly had a brilliant new idea: We were all going to Wampir Ski Resort for a week of "snowy fun."

I'd never skied before, but I was willing to give downhill a try. Matt had gone snowboarding a few times with a club from his school and wanted to get better at it. We both loved sports, so how hard could it be?

"Hey, Dad." I figured I'd try asking one more time. "How much longer?"

I expected him to say, "Soon," but instead he said, "We're here."

"Huh?" I sat up straight and rubbed the thin coat of breathy steam off the van window with a corner of my sweater. I looked out. It was early afternoon, but the entire mountainside seemed to have a dark cloud hovering over it, which made it seem spooky—in an awesome way!

"Matt!" I grabbed his arm to get his attention.

He had to lean over the body bag and then over me to peer out the window. "Wow," he echoed my excitement.

The lodge was old. Run-down. And creepy. It was three stories high with tall, imposing spires, like a castle. The road to the front door was covered with a thick layer of snow.

I squinted through the window, pressing my nose against the cold glass for a better look. Part of the roof appeared to have crumbled under the weight of snow buildup and the huge icicles that hung off the side of the building. They looked like a row of deadly tiger fangs. All along the front of the place, dark gray paint was peeling, and the steep porch was completely caved in on one side.

"That's not at all what I expected!" Matt cheered. "We're going to have the best vacation ever." This time when he raised his hand for a high five, I smacked it. "The ski lodge looks like a haunted mansion!"

"Forget resurrecting your dead body," I said. "We're going ghost hunting!"

"Yeah," Matt agreed. He rested a hand on his large duffel. "We don't need Frankenstein's monster. It's just my snowboard anyway. And some smelly socks."

"You never fooled me." I laughed. "That's what I thought." The hard lump I'd felt when I smacked it must have been the snowboard's bindings.

Suddenly, our van turned away from the eerie lodge and down another road.

"Wait! We need to go that way," I said, tapping my hand against the van window.

"Turn left!" Matt told his dad. "Left!"

"You're joking, right?" my dad asked us, looking toward the ski lodge and then directing his eyes back to the GPS. "You two are always messing around, trying to scare each other. Well, you can't fool the grown-ups. We know where we're going." He pointed to the GPS. "And it's not Creepy Hollow over there."

"You're looking at the old lodge," Roberto, Matt's dad, said with a chuckle. "That place should be condemned."

I could hear the smile in my dad's voice when he said, "Who'd want to stay there when we can stay"—he paused for a bit of drama as another building came into view—"here?"

Down a long, freshly plowed driveway was a gleaming, brand-new three-story resort. The palatial building was painted white with gold trim. The windows shone with pretty ice crystals. Glowing lamps lit the path to the two large, intricately carved front doors.

"Bummer," Matt said, glancing over his shoulder at the old lodge before turning his attention to the new one.

"Ditto," I said with a nod.

When Matt's dad stopped the car, a tall man in a crisp blue coat and black brimmed bellman's cap opened the door to help us all out.

Our dads went in to the reception desk. Our moms and Chloe gathered their handbags. Matt swung himself out of the backseat.

I hung out a minute while the tall man dug out Matt's duffel. He didn't even struggle with it. In his large hands, the heavy bag that had crushed my legs for hours seemed light as a feather.

Finally, my path was clear. I was the last one out of the van. By the time I got out, everyone else was already inside the lodge having a welcome cup of hot cocoa.

Everyone, that was, except Matt. He'd waited for me.

"Brrr." I shivered. It was cold. The freezing wind whipped through my light sweater. I hadn't thought to leave out warmer clothes. I looked at our luggage piled on the bellman's cart and wondered which suitcase held my heavy coat and gloves. I was going to need them before I went outside again.

"Hang on, Zo." Matt held me back for a second. I could tell he wanted a moment to take in the resort and the ski slopes in the distance. "I'm really excited to be here."

I wanted my coat but decided to give him a minute.

"Check it out!" He pointed out the last straggling skiers coming down the slopes for the final afternoon run. They carried torches to indicate the end of the day.

"I can't wait to hit the slopes tomorrow," I told him. A whole week of skiing, snowboarding, and adventure lay before us.

"Miss Lancaster and Mr. Ortiz, if you'll please follow me." With a tip of his hat and a tight smile that didn't reach his eyes, the bellman held out a hand, ushering us toward the sparkling new Wampir Ski Resort and Lodge. He paused at the door, taking his time to open it. Just before we entered, the bellman said in a heavy foreign accent, "Velcome to Vampir."

Chapter Two

"Dinner's in forty-five minutes," my mom said. She was busy unpacking Chloe's things into a small dresser sandwiched between two twin beds in a tiny bedroom. "Make sure you wear something nice. The dining hall at the lodge is on the formal side. No jeans!"

I actually liked having an excuse to dress up a little. It was too cold for a dress or skirt, but the shimmery black leggings and fluffy green sweater outfit I'd packed seemed like it would be perfect. I changed quickly and tried fixing my hair, but after having been in a ponytail all day, it had that weird crimp in it when I took it down. Ponytail it was.

The cabin we'd rented was small but had enough space for both families to be together comfortably. Chloe and I shared a small bedroom with its own bathroom, while Matt would sleep on the pullout couch in the living room. There was a cute little kitchen, but we hadn't bought groceries yet. Once we did, we'd have breakfast in the cabin each morning and maybe a few dinners.

Matt and I stood together in front of the large sliding-glass door next to his sofa bed waiting for our parents to finish getting ready for dinner. Matt had changed into a nice pair of tan pants and a sweater. He kept tugging at the neck of the sweater. I could tell it was bothering him to be wearing something other than a sweatshirt.

"The ski slopes look amazing," he said between tugs. There was nothing blocking the view of the mountain face from our cabin.

We'd seen the last ski run and the lifts were closed now, but I could see the direction they went, winding up the mountain before disappearing into the heavy gray snow clouds at the top.

"Look this way." Matt put his hand on my shoulder and turned me around.

"Oh, cool!" From this angle, I could see the ticket booth and the ski rental shop. Across the road stood the old lodge. Now that it was getting dark, the place looked even more run-down and spooky than when we'd first seen it from the car.

I squinted at the house, staring at a dark spot

in the upper window, when suddenly the shadow moved.

"Did you see that?" Matt asked excitedly.

He'd seen the shadow move too.

"I don't know," I said cautiously. "Maybe." I wasn't sure I'd actually seen anything at all. "It could have been a trick of the light—something with the sunset reflecting on the shattered glass."

"There's only one way to find out. Let's go check it out," Matt said.

"Do you think we have time to go now? Dinner's really soon."

"Now is perfect. It's about to get totally dark out there. At least now there's still some light."

Matt was right. It was getting dark fast. If we were going to go to the old lodge, it had to be right away.

I went into the bedroom to ask Mom. She was brushing her shoulder-length blond hair. Everyone said I looked a lot like her, while Chloe had inherited my dad's darker skin and hair.

"Can I go with Matt to check out the lodge?" I asked. I left "lodge" intentionally vague. If I got in trouble for letting her think I meant the new one, then I could always play it off like, "Oh, you thought I meant the new lodge. That's funny because I meant the old one."

"I wanna go with Zoe," Chloe whined.

"Don't you have to get ready for dinner?" I asked her.

"Your sister's right, sweetie," my mom said. "We have to get you dressed for dinner."

"Can we make snow angels outside before you go?" Chloe replied.

She doesn't give up easily.

"It's kind of dark for snow angels," I told her. "Plus, like Mom said, it's almost time for dinner. Maybe another time?"

That seemed to satisfy her. She began rummaging through the drawers my mom had just neatly unpacked her clothes into.

My mom sighed and turned to look at me directly. "If I let you go with Matt now, do you promise to take Chloe to make snow angels tomorrow after skiing?"

"Deal. Done." Hopefully by morning, Chloe would have forgotten all about it.

"Meet us in the dining room for dinner in fifteen minutes," Mom told me. Then she added, "We are talking about the new lodge, right?"

Ah, drat. Mom was a mind reader. She had this uncanny ability to know what I was *really* thinking.

"Of course," I said, trying to keep the disappointment out of my voice. The old lodge would have to wait.

I looked at the time on my cell phone. "Dinner in fifteen. Got it." Then I noticed my phone had no service. "I wonder if the lodge has Wi-Fi," I said to myself as I went to meet up with Matt, who'd been having a similar conversation with his parents.

"They don't want us to stray from the lodge," he said as we hurried outside into the bitter cold. "Dad said 'new lodge,' like he knew where we really wanted to go."

"They know us too well." I laughed. "We'll make it to the old lodge another time." I raised an eyebrow. "Soon."

My coat was warm, but my nose was frozen. I stuffed my gloved hands into my jacket with a mental note to take a scarf for skiing tomorrow.

"It's okay. We can do some research on that old place before we check it out," I continued as we walked toward the entrance to the lodge. "What do you think we saw in the window? We should find out if anyone died—"

I was about to say more, when instead of letting me go through the door first, Matt pushed himself past me and let the door slam closed behind him.

"No!" I shouted, realizing he was going to hold the door closed to keep me out. He held the handles tight and laughed hysterically while I struggled to pull the door open.

I wouldn't ever tell him, but I thought it was funny too. He'd tricked me, and I'd fallen for it. But then a blast of winter air whipped snow off the lodge's roof and into my hair. It was so cold! I leaned over a low snowbank to brush it off, then swung around, giving Matt the evil eye through the door's smoky glass. This wasn't funny anymore.

"Let me in!" I called out to him. "It's freezing out here."

"Oh, all right." He reluctantly opened the door to let me in, teasing, "You should have seen your face—that was classic!"

"I'll get you for that one, Mateo," I warned. "You'd better watch your back." He didn't know it, but I didn't mean in the future. I meant now. When he turned, I smacked him with a snowball right between the shoulder blades. "Ha." I clapped my hands together, feeling satisfied.

"We're even," he told me, brushing wet snow off his neck. I heard him add in a low whisper, "For now."

I laughed. "Do your best," I challenged. "But be on the lookout. This fancy new lodge might not be scary, but I am!"

There was never an official truce between Matt and me. When we were downstairs by the spa and hot tub, he pretended he was looking for a pencil, then jumped out of an empty conference room to scare me.

"Bah, humbug," I told him. "Not scary."

We went upstairs to a small gaming room with a fire in the corner. When he wasn't looking, I knocked over a rack of pool cues, thinking the noise would scare him. But it didn't.

By the time we got back to the main reception area of the lodge, we'd given up. We crashed down onto a very plush, soft couch in front of a large wood-burning fire. The overstuffed pillows made a gassy sound. He laughed while I rolled my eyes at him.

"I hope the slopes are awesome because this place is kind of boring," Matt said, resting his head back against the fluffy cushions.

"You think the Wampir Resort is boring?" a woman sitting nearby asked. She leaned around the high wings of a small velvet chair. I hadn't noticed her when we came in.

The lady seemed out of place in her glamorous, high-necked, old-fashioned gown and small veiled hat. She was thin, with long hair and brown eyes— no, yellow eyes. No, they were definitely green. They looked like they kept changing.

"Come with me," she said, rising. "I'd like to show you something special."

"Uh," I stalled. As much as I was willing to sneak away, play pranks, and pop out of hidden corners to scare my best friend, I didn't think going off with a stranger was a smart idea.

"Have you seen the lodge library?" she asked, moving in closer to us.

"Library?" Matt asked, curious. "There's a library in the lodge?"

We hadn't seen one on the resort map.

"Certainly you've noticed that there is barely phone reception and no Internet service at the lodge," she said, looking at me with eyes that now seemed to be violet.

"Oh, we've noticed," Matt said.

The woman nodded sympathetically. "It's quiet here late at night. If you can't play with your phones, what will you do? Did you bring books to read?"

She had a good point. Neither one of us had thought to bring books. We had both thought we would be able to just download books to read.

"Does the library have any scary stories?" Matt asked. "That's what I like to read. The scarier, the better."

"Follow me," the woman told us. "I'm certain you will find exactly what you need."

Since we weren't leaving the lodge, I figured it was okay to go along.

The library was a small room off the main lobby. There were two plush reading chairs, a small desk with pens and paper, and a tall shelf of books.

At the top of the shelf was a sign.

It read: "Give One/Take One."

"What does that mean?" I asked the woman, wondering if she worked at the lodge.

"If you brought a book from home, you should leave it here and take a new one," she replied.

"But I didn't bring anything," I said sadly, wishing I had.

"I didn't bring anything either," Matt told her.

"I was thinking I'd be using my laptop to watch sports."

The woman's eyes seemed to shift to black as she said, "Don't worry. Just take what you want. When you reach the end of the story, you can put it back here before you return home."

"Okay," Matt said. "Sounds good."

We began to look through the shelves starting at the very top, going down row by row. There were romance novels, cowboy novels, and a lot of mysteries. But no scary stories.

"This stinks," Matt said after reaching the bottom shelf. "Nothing looks scary!"

"I don't think you've looked hard enough," the woman said from behind us.

I jumped back a little. She moved so quietly that she surprised me.

Matt laughed, but I could tell he'd been surprised as well.

She reached up to the top shelf, in the middle of the row, and pulled out a strange-looking book.

I swore I had looked in that spot. How had I missed that book? It was an antique leather-bound journal with a small brass clasp. The most fascinating part was that the cover had several strange triangles etched into the leather. They'd been painted gold at some point, but the color had faded with age.

The woman handed the book to Matt, and as it passed by me, I smelled a sharp metallic odor rising from the leather. Matt opened the book and set it on the small desk so we could both look inside. The pages were made of a thick yellowed paper, with a slight tinge of brown around the edges.

On the first page were the words:

Tales from the Scaremaster

But beneath that title, the rest of the page was blank.

I flipped a few pages. "They're all blank."

A few pages in, I noticed some light red smears on the paper. I pointed at the stains.

"It's definitely blood," Matt said in a confident voice, as if he were an expert on bloodstains.

"You're just trying to scare me," I told him. "It's not working."

"Since you like scary stories," the woman advised, "perhaps you could write your own?" Over her shoulder there was a small window that looked out toward the old, run-down Wampir lodge. "There might be something around here that would inspire you...." she hinted, glancing back at me and Matt.

She handed me a pen from the desk. "You could start now." She said, her voice low and even. It was a bit hypnotic, like a magician I'd once seen at a fair.

I had the strangest feeling that the woman wasn't going to let us leave the library until we'd written something. Not like she was locking us in, but rather, she wanted us to write so badly she'd stay with us until we did.

Matt told me, "You start the story, and I'll jump in when I have an idea."

"Okay," I agreed. Not wanting to let the woman down, since she was the one who'd discovered the journal, I leaned over the page and wrote:

Once upon a time, Mateo Ortiz
and Zoe Lancaster were looking
for adventure in the Wampir Ski
Resort and Lodge.

"Wait!" Matt suddenly pointed at the page. "Look!"

Under my writing, there were new words. I hadn't written them. And neither had Matt.

It said:

*Looking for a scare,
are you? The Scaremaster won't
disappoint you. You shouldn't
have started this story.
Now I get to finish it!*

Chapter Three

"You wrote that." I turned to Matt. "How did you do that? Some new trick you learned? Was she in on it?" As much as I didn't want to admit that I was spooked, I was. How had he done that?

"I didn't...." Matt turned around. "She..." The woman who'd shown us the book was gone. Matt looked totally shocked. He wasn't that good of an actor.

"It had to be her," Matt insisted. "She's the one who wanted us to write in it so badly!"

"Where'd she go?" I looked out the library door. "We gotta find her and ask her how she did that." We ran into the main lobby area. She wasn't in the chair where we'd first seen her. She wasn't at the reception desk. She wasn't anywhere!

"Did we imagine her?" I asked Matt, who was awkwardly holding the strange journal in front of him. He seemed both a little afraid to put it down and scared to hold it too close.

"Imagine who?" a voice cut in. It was Chloe. "Whatcha got, Matt?"

He looked down at his hands as if surprised to discover he still held the journal. "A book," he said simply.

"Can I read it?" Chloe asked. Her hair was in high pigtails that bobbed as she skipped closer to Matt and the journal.

"No way," Matt said quickly. I knew he didn't mean to sound so harsh; it was just that we didn't know anything about the journal yet. We needed more time to check it out. Time without Chloe looking over our shoulders.

If I tried to hide the book, it would just make my sister curious. I didn't want that, so I gave her just enough information to stop her from asking any more questions.

"It's a book of terrifying stories," I told her, prying the book from Matt's tight grip. I flashed her the first page in way to disguise that the book was basically blank. "See?" I used my arm to block as much of the page as I could. I only wanted her to see the title.

"'*Tales from the Scaremaster*,'" Chloe read slowly. "That doesn't seem *that* scary."

"Oh no?" I said, raising an eyebrow and teasing her. "This book has the scariest stories ever told." I raised that eyebrow even higher and whispered, "And the best part...they're all true."

"Really?" Chloe looked up at me. "No way. You're kidding, right?" Even though she was wearing her coat, she gave a little shiver.

I shrugged. "Honestly, I don't know yet," I told her. "We just got it from the library." I pointed in the direction of the bookshelves. "Maybe after dinner you can go find something to read too." We'd seen kids' books on the bottom shelf.

"Nah," Chloe said, shaking her head. "I've got my comic books." My sister loved superheroes. Her comic collection could have filled Matt's body bag/duffel and more. I wasn't a huge fan of comics. But if the Scaremaster's journal ended up being a bust, we could check out what she brought.

Mom and Dad and Matt's parents came to join us. They'd been over at the activities desk arranging the next day on the slopes.

"You ready?" Matt's dad asked us.

I quickly took off my coat and slid the journal under it. I wrapped the jacket around the book and said, "Yep. Now we are." I gave Matt a wink, and we went in to dinner.

My grilled salmon was good, but I didn't take the time to enjoy it. Matt kept kicking me under the table. And when he wasn't doing that, he was asking me whether I was done yet.

The instant he swallowed his last bite of pasta, Matt stood. He stretched and yawned. "I'm beat. Ready to hit the couch." He tugged at my arm. "Zoe will walk back with me, okay?"

My dad gave me an odd look. "I thought you wanted cake," he said. "It's German chocolate, your favorite."

That was my favorite, and I *did* want dessert.

Coming to stand behind my chair, Matt snatched up my jacket. I could tell he was being careful not to reveal the book that was wrapped up inside it. "She can have cake another night," he said. "Come on, Zo. Time to go."

"I—" I knew Matt wanted time to check out the book before everyone else came to the cabin. I wanted time too, but I also wanted cake!

"Oh, all right," I gave in. "The prince needs his beauty sleep, I suppose." If he kneed the back of my seat one more time, I was going to turn around and stab him with my fork.

I asked Mom and Dad, "Do you mind if I walk him back?"

"We were going to stay in the lodge for a while," Mom said. "There's going to be a folk music band and cocoa by the big fireplace."

That was actually good news. It meant Matt and I had longer to investigate the Scaremaster's tales.

"Bummer to miss the band," I said, trying to sound as disappointed as possible. "Maybe they'll come again later this week," I said, holding up my crossed fingers.

My mom, psychic as she is, laughed. "You two have fun. Don't get in trouble." She meant that last bit.

"We won't," I told her. "I promise."

How much trouble could we get into? We were

going to check out a book that wrote stories by itself. What could possibly go wrong?

We sat together on Matt's bed, which was now still a couch. The book was between us, half on my lap, half on Matt's.

"How do you think it works?" I asked, twirling a pen between my fingers.

"It's possessed," Matt said, adding, "Duh."

It was like we'd been preparing for this book our whole lives. All that scaring each other. All those pranks and tricks and jokes. They had led us to this. We'd found a book that was meant to scare us!

"Possessed? That sounds awesome," I told Matt, hoping with all my heart that he was right. "What do we do? How do we know for sure?"

Matt looked at the pen in my hand. "Write something."

I'd already written a start to a story, but I didn't want my own tale. If this book was really possessed, I wanted to hear a Scaremaster scary story. I mean, that's what he promised, right?

It was still there, written on the page like a contract:

Looking for a scare, are you? The Scaremaster won't disappoint you.

I trembled, not with fear but rather with excitement, as I wrote:

We're looking for a scare.

For a long moment, nothing happened. I held my breath. Beside me, Matt's leg was twitching.

"You're shaking the book," I said, not looking away from the page. Thinking I saw a little ink dot on one of those red blood-looking stains, I bent over the journal for a closer look. "Is that handwriting?"

"I don't think so," Matt said, putting his face near mine as we started at the page together. "I think it's a smudge. It looks like—"

When actual writing appeared, we both jumped and we bumped heads.

"Ack!" Matt said, pulling back so fast, his hand accidentally knocked the book off the couch.

"Ouch!" I shouted, grabbing my head with two hands. "You've got a hard head," I told Matt, rubbing the sore spot. "That's gonna bruise."

"I know," he said with a small smile. "Lucky, right? Never had a concussion."

"Bragger," I said. Concussions were common in soccer, when a player hit the ball with her head like I did. I was really careful, though, and took healing seriously.

Careful not to bump him again, I reached past Matt to grab the book from under the coffee table. I set it back between us.

"Read it," Matt said. "Use your spooky voice, Zoe."

I did have a good spooky voice. In a low, breathy tone, I read, " 'Fact or fiction?' "

"It's a question," I told Matt, raising my eyes from the page. "What does he mean?"

"I've got this," Matt said, pulling the Scaremaster's journal toward him. "He's going to tell us a story. Do you want one that's true, based in fact? Or would you rather he make something up?"

I could not believe we were sitting in a cabin at the Wampir Resort talking to a possessed book! Even if it turned out to be someone's joke, it was a good one. I was going to enjoy every minute of it.

"What's scarier?" I asked Matt. "I think we should go with the one that will frighten us more."

"Ask the Scaremaster," Matt told me, turning the book toward me. "It's his story."

I wrote:

> You promised to scare us.
> We'll take the scarier one.

I'll tell you the story of the Wampir Resort.

Instinctively Matt and I both glanced through the big window in the direction of the old lodge. It was dark outside. There was a glow from the moonlight on the packed snow, and we could see a dusting of fresh snowflakes drifting down. We couldn't see the old lodge in the blackness, but there was a distinct light coming from where it would have been. A flickering yellow pinpoint, like a flashlight or candle, was shining through a window on the third floor.

I leaned into Matt. "This is really happening,"

I whispered, feeling the goose bumps on his arm pressed against the goose bumps on my own.

"So cool," he said, tapping the journal with a finger. "Zoe, say okay. Tell him we want to hear the story."

"Do you think this story will be fact or fiction?" I asked Matt, giving one last glance toward the old lodge. Now it was completely dark. Whatever or whoever we'd seen was gone.

Matt shrugged. "It doesn't matter if it's true or not. As long as it's scary."

I wrote:

Scare us.

The Scaremaster replied:

Oh, I will....

Chapter Four

Tales from the Scaremaster

Night at Wampir Resort

December 28, 1882

Count Frederic Wampir held the creamy white invitation
in his hand. At the top of the stationery was his family
crest, two red dots above a scrawled letter <u>W</u>. The <u>W</u> was
emblazoned in gold, of course. He'd had the gold leaf from
his own treasury crushed to dust. It was expensive to put the
crest on each and every invitation with fine lines of the
precious metal, but it was worth the cost. Because tonight
was the most important night of Count Frederic's
life.

  He had handwritten the invitations himself.

Please join me this evening for a special celebration.

The grand opening of the
Wampir Ski Resort and Lodge

Dinner will be served at
8:00 p.m.

Dancing to follow

Count Frederic loved parties. It had been a long time since he'd hosted, or even attended one. Since leaving his native Transylvania, he'd wandered the globe, unable to stay for long in any one place. There was never a reason to celebrate. Fear forced the count to look over his shoulder at every turn. Anxiety kept him awake at night.

As long as <u>she</u> lived, he had to stay alert. Never sleep. He had to watch his back and keep constant vigil. If she found him, Frederic knew his fate.

His mother was a monster. She roamed the streets at night, searching for a way to satisfy her insatiable hunger.

As the oldest son, it was his responsibility to follow in his mother's footsteps.

Count Frederic Wampir rejected this legacy, and so he ran. He moved from place to place with the endless fear that she would find him. And make him just like her.

Count Frederic set the last invitation on his desk and sealed it with thick red wax. The invitations would be hand-delivered room by room by the hotel bellman. The rooms were all occupied for the week. The hotel was full.

Tonight was a special occasion.

A year earlier, his brother had sent word that his mother was dead.

A stake had pierced her heart.

The curse was over.

He was free.

Construction on the lodge had begun that very day. And tonight, he would celebrate.

"What's frightening about that? It's just about a guy having a party," I told Matt as the flowery writing faded from the page. "The Scaremaster's tale isn't so scary."

"Obviously, the count didn't want to become a vampire like his mom," Matt said, staring down at the now blank page in the journal. "And he didn't."

"What fun is that?" I picked up the pen and twirled it between my fingers. "I'd be way more scared if he'd gotten bitten."

"Yeah. Then went out to terrorize the lodge guests at night," Matt agreed. "That would be better."

I wrote in the journal:

> Not so scary. We think he
> should have turned into
> a vampire.

The Scaremaster wrote back immediately:

> **The story isn't over.**
> **Turn the page.**

"Oh. Oops." I laughed a little as I noticed that, in fact, the Scaremaster's story continued on the next page.

In the ballroom at the Wampir Resort, tables were set with the finest china. Crystal glasses twinkled in the warm glow from the huge chandeliers. The band played familiar songs from the count's homeland, and everyone danced.

It was perfect.

That was, until the guest from room 22 disappeared. He was a dentist from the city who'd gone out for a "breath of fresh air" but never returned.

An hour later, a chef went missing from the kitchen.

Some guests reported hearing a scuffle and a door slam. But who scuffled and who slammed the door? No one knew.

When the woman from the newspaper, there to report on the gala, left her husband sitting alone, the count knew something was terribly wrong. She would never have missed the party on purpose. Reporting on it was her job, after all.

Frederic frantically rushed table to table, counting each and every guest. Then he closed the large ballroom doors, locking everyone inside.

"Please continue to enjoy your evening," the count told his guests, pretending that everything was all right.

They would be safe inside, he assured himself. The ballroom was well sealed, and no one could get in or out.

He ordered the band to play "happy" tunes and asked the waitstaff to serve dessert.

Then, while the guests were distracted, he snuck out the kitchen door, locking it behind him.

After his mother's passing, Count Frederic had relaxed. He no longer took precautions. He'd built the lodge thinking there was no reason to fear anything or anyone ever again.

Until tonight. Now his entire body was consumed with fear. It was freezing outside, and yet, a bead of sweat rolled across his forehead as he walked around to the front door of the lodge, scanning the darkness for movement.

There? Was that a noise? A movement in the dark? No. His head turned side to side. There? No.

After a long while, he determined that there was nothing outside and went back to the ballroom through the kitchen door. He would continue the celebration as if nothing were wrong. Perhaps the few missing people had gone away on their own. It was possible, though it didn't seem likely. He pushed the alternatives from his mind and entered the ballroom.

Stepping inside, Count Frederic immediately noticed that the music had changed. It was no longer the happy dance tunes he had requested. Rather, now the band was playing a slow march with a steady rhythm and clashing chords. It was a song of his youth. He hadn't heard it since he'd left home.

His body shook with a chill. The song, the coolness of the

air, the glazed look in his guests' eyes—it all could only mean one thing.

She was back.

He found her in a red velvet chair on a platform in the center of the room. Neither the chair nor the platform had been there when he'd set up the room. She must have brought them herself when she arrived.

Count Frederic Wampir straightened his back, consciously exposing his long neck. He tilted his head to the side as he said in icy tones, "Hello, Mother." His accent thickened, and his tone deepened as he greeted her, "Velcome to Vampir."

"Definitely scarier now," I told Matt. "Especially since that's the way the old bellman greeted us when we first arrived."

"Just a coincidence," Matt assured me. "We told the Scaremaster to scare us, so he's working hard at it."

"Are you scared?" I asked Matt.

"Nah," Matt told me. "Are you?"

"Nah," I echoed, though there was something nagging me. I wasn't scared, but I did feel a little… out of sorts. I reached out to turn the journal's page. "That can't be the end, can it?"

"I hope not," Matt said. "It might not be the scariest story I ever heard, but still, I want to know if the count got turned into a vampire by his mom. If the guests lived. If everyone became vampires. What happened next? There's a lot left to find out!"

"Let's see if there's more." I began to flip the page when suddenly the cabin door burst open with a blast of cold air.

"ZOE! MATT!" Chloe rushed into the cabin. She had snowflakes in her hair. Without closing the door behind her, she immediately began tossing off her warm clothes. Her jacket, gloves, hat, and scarf all fell into a pile. "The band was so good!" she announced. "They played all these old songs. I never heard any of them before. Some were in a strange language."

"Dutch, I think," Matt's mom said, coming into the cabin with the other parents.

"Romanian," my dad suggested.

"Could have been Hungarian or German," Matt's dad said. He shrugged and laughed. "We probably should have asked."

"Wherever the songs were from, the band was terrific, and we even danced a little." My mom turned to Chloe and pointed at the clothing pile.

"Pick up your mess, please. There are hooks by the door."

"Ah, man," Chloe complained Then, as she gathered her things, she started to hum. It was the oddest song that I'd ever heard. Like a march, with clashing notes and a strangely steady rhythm.

My head spun around to look at Matt. His eyes were wide as he stared at Chloe.

"Where'd you hear that?" I asked my sister. "That song? Did you know it before we came to Wampir?"

"Nope," Chloe said, slipping her jacket onto a hook. She started back toward the couch. "Weren't you listening? I told you! The band played songs from some other place. They were awesome!" She added, "The bellman from the lodge was there. He taught us dance steps!"

"Like a folk dance?" I asked.

"Exactly!" Chloe said, and she showed us a few moves.

Just before Chloe reached the sofa, I quickly shut the Scaremaster's book. I didn't know if there was another page in his story, but there was no time to keep reading.

Matt gave me an intense glare with his eyebrows raised. I knew what he meant. We both wanted to keep the mysterious journal a secret. So I leaned back and tucked the journal behind the couch cushion.

"Hey, Zo," Matt whispered, "promise you won't read the book without me, okay?"

"You either," I said, and we shook pinkies to seal the agreement.

"Kids," my mom cut in, addressing not just Chloe but me too. "It's bedtime. We have an early day tomorrow."

"Skiing!" Chloe cheered. "I can't wait!" She swiveled on her socks and marched off toward the bedroom, humming the strange tune she'd heard earlier.

A second later, Matt's mom told him, "You too, young man. Say good night to Zoe."

"Got it," he replied. Then Matt slipped me the Scaremaster's journal. "Hide this in your closet, okay?" he whispered.

I took the book, tucked it under my sweater, and started off toward the room I shared with Chloe. Suddenly, I had an important thought.

Hustling back to the couch, I leaned over and whispered to Matt, "What language do they speak in Transylvania?"

"I wish I had Internet," he said, "but I can guess. Dutch? Hungarian? German?"

"Romanian?" I asked. "I bet that's the most likely, though that part of Europe has so many people moving around, it might be a mix of all of them."

"One of those," he said. "The song Chloe was humming sounds like it might have been the same as the one in the Scaremaster's story. Could it be the same song the band played at the grand opening of the old lodge?"

"Yes," I admitted. I took a deep breath and stared down at the journal in my hands. "The Scaremaster's story just got a whole lot scarier."

Chapter Five

I stashed the book in the bedroom closet, behind a suitcase. Then I threw a couple sweaters over it for good measure. Chloe was using the dresser drawers, so the closet was all mine. No one would ever find the book there.

The Scaremaster's story was done for the night. I looked forward to what he'd offer up tomorrow.

I changed for bed.

The instant my head hit the pillows, the dream began.

My mother was a bat. It wasn't like she was wearing a sign or had any special markings; I just knew it was her.

"Mom!" I cried out, hands raised toward the sky. She was circling our rented cabin, ducking through trees and flitting playfully in the moonlight over my head. "Mom!" I shouted. "What are you doing?"

Suddenly, she flew away. I chased after her, running as fast as I could from the cabin, down the icy road toward the old lodge. "Where are you going? Come back!"

The bat gave off a high-pitched wail, then flew with strong wings into the run-down lodge through a broken window on the second floor.

I looked around. I was alone.

Suddenly, without actually walking into the lodge, I found myself inside the lobby.

Ahead of me was a broad staircase that rose to the second floor with wide steps that narrowed as they reached the upper landing. All along the stairs were portraits. In the shadows of darkness, I could see they were paintings of both men and women in old-fashioned clothing. Most of the paintings had spiderwebs in the corners of the frames. In many, the canvases were torn. All the portraits were hanging crooked.

To the right of the stairway was what appeared to be the old guest registration area. There was a long desk, and small, crumbling key hooks lined the far wall. To the left, broken doors with shattered inlaid stained glass hung off their hinges, marking the entrance to a room that was probably once very beautiful.

"Mom?" I called out, rubbing my arms from the cold.

Where was my warm coat? There was a feeling that what I was seeing wasn't real, and yet, I was freezing. I realized that I must have forgotten my jacket at the cabin. I'd been so desperate to find Mom that I'd gone outside wearing only pajamas and flip-flops.

Breathing into my hands to warm them, I stepped toward that large room to my left, immediately recognizing that this was, long ago, the Wampir Resort grand ballroom. I pushed through what remained of the termite-eaten doors and entered the space.

The ballroom itself was a vast, empty room. The enormous windows that faced the slopes were either clouded with age or cracked. The wind drifted through those damaged windows and the room's temperature seemed to fall with each gust.

I shivered but wasn't sure if it was from the cold or from being alone in the spooky old lodge.

"Mom?" I called out again. Several bats squealed

at me from the rafters. Were they happy to see me? Or warning me to run away?

I pushed back my nerves. I liked scary things, and this old lodge was the most frightening place I'd ever been. It would be a lot more exciting if Matt were here.

With a mental promise to come back with him in the daytime, I looked around. In this moment, I didn't feel like exploring. I had an overwhelming desire to find my mom and bring her safely back to the cabin.

"Mom?" I called again, looking up toward the ceiling. There had only been a few bats in the rafters a moment ago. Now there were hundreds. They formed a squealing, shrieking black cloud above my head.

I could no longer see where one bat separated from the others. They were blended. How would I ever find my mother in the crowd?

"Mom!" Panic began boiling in my blood. "Where are you?"

"I'm here, Zoe." A woman's voice echoed through the room. "Come, Zoe. Come to Mother."

"Mom?" The woman's voice was familiar and yet entirely different from my mother's. I stepped farther into the ballroom.

"Whoa!" I gasped. I blinked and rubbed my eyes.

The ballroom, which had been dark, cold, and drafty moments ago, was now lavishly decorated for a party. Round tables circled a glimmering wooden dance floor. The tables were set with candles, flowers, and the finest china I'd ever seen.

"Do you like it?" the woman's voice called to me. "Would you like an invitation to the party?"

In my heart, I knew this was a trap. I knew I needed to run away, but still, I needed to find my mom.

In the center of the room, just as the Scaremaster had described it, a red velvet chair appeared. It was similar to the one the woman who had given us the journal had been sitting in at the new lodge.

"No way," I breathed as I moved closer. But it *was* similar. Perhaps even the same.

The woman in the chair rose and turned around. Finally, I could see her face.

This wasn't the woman who'd shown us the library. It wasn't my mother either. This was a woman I'd never seen before. She was young, maybe in her early thirties, with long dark hair that reached the middle of her back. Her red party gown had a high lace neck, and she was wearing long white gloves.

Is this a ghost? I wondered. Matt and I had already figured that the old lodge was probably haunted. Again, I wished he were with me. He'd have been so excited. Here I was, face-to-face with a real ghost! I couldn't wait to tell Matt all about it, but first...

"Where's my mom?" I asked the woman. "Tell me," I demanded.

The bats above her head squealed loudly.

"Darling, Zoe. I am your mother," the woman said, raising her arms to invite me in for a hug. "And you are my daughter."

"No! You aren't my mother!" I screamed, in a voice I didn't recognize as my own. "No. No. No!"

"Zoe!" Chloe sat up in the other bed. She tossed her pillow at my head. "You're having a nightmare. Wake up!"

Pushing Chloe's pillow off my face, I rubbed my eyes. I felt disoriented. It took me a long moment to realize I was in the rented cabin, not in the old lodge. My eyelids felt heavy. I blinked rapidly until the room came clearly into view.

"Whew," I said, taking a deep breath. "You're right. Just a nightmare." I laughed at myself. "That story must have been scarier than I thought."

"You read a scary story before bed?" Chloe rolled on her side to face me. "Mom says never to do that. That's how you get nightmares."

"I know," I said. Mom warned me all the time, but I never listened. Then again, I'd never had a nightmare like this one before.

Shaking off the bad dream, I gave Chloe back her pillow and leaned into my own comfortable sheets, pulling up my comforter. I closed my eyes, willing myself to think about skiing and snow and other happy thoughts.

"Zoe," Chloe said with a yawn, "turn off the night-light."

"Night-light?" I sat up in bed. There wasn't a night-light in the room. And yet, Chloe was right. There was a strong glow filling the room. It came from the dresser between the two beds.

"Flashlight. Night-light. Phone," Chloe complained, rolling away from me. "Whatever you just turned on, turn it off. It's too bright. I can't sleep with it on."

"There must be a light on a timer." I climbed out of bed. "I'll take care of it."

When I saw the source of the glow, I had to stop myself from screaming again. I pinched myself to make sure that this time I was awake.

"What is going on?" I muttered. This was worse than my nightmare. Much scarier.

There, on the dresser, was the Scaremaster's journal. And it was glowing.

"I know I put this in the closet," I said aloud, glancing to the closet door. It was shut, like when I'd closed it. "Impossible." My heartbeat sped up as I stared at the Scaremaster's book. "What's this doing here?"

"Shhh..." Chloe groaned. "No talking."

I bit my tongue to keep quiet.

I didn't want to worry Chloe, but this was too weird, even for me!

Tipping my head, I considered the situation. I didn't know what might happen if I touched the journal while it was lit up like that. Would I be electrocuted? Sucked into the pages? I'd read too many scary stories and knew this was a bad omen.

This was one of those plot points where the evil thing began to take over. I didn't want to be the first victim.

Holding my breath and with very slow movements, I lightly tapped one finger on the book's cover.

The glowing light went out.

The room was cast into an eerie darkness.

Chloe moaned sleepily, "Thanks." Moments later, I could tell from her heavy breathing that she'd already fallen back to sleep.

Now that the book looked once again like a normal old journal, I felt confident that I could touch it safely. I scooped the book up and fled the bedroom to where Matt snored on the sofa bed.

"This thing is giving me nightmares," I told him, shaking his shoulder. "Matt." I was whispering so as not to wake the others. "Matt. I'm telling you the Scaremaster's journal really is possessed."

"Go away," Matt told me, pushing off my hand and pulling the blanket over his head. "No pranks while I'm sleeping."

"I'm not kidding," I said, tugging down his covers to reveal his face. "I had bad, bad nightmares about my mom turning into a bat."

"Your mom was a bat?" Matt snorted. "That's

funny. Everyone knows she hates to fly." He pried the blanket out of my hands. "We're hitting the slopes early. I need energy. Go to sleep."

"I can't!" I held out the book toward him. "It's not just the nightmares. This thing moves and glows."

Matt sat up in bed. "Zoe, cut it out. You *can't* scare me. Give it up."

"I'm not pulling a prank." I held up one hand like I was taking a vow. "I promise."

Matt stared at me for a long moment. His hair was standing on end on one side of his head and was smooshed down on the other side. "Fine." He took the book. "Leave it here. If I have nightmares or the book bursts into flames, I'll come get you." He shoved it under the sofa bed. "Now can I go back to sleep? I was dreaming about grinding rails in fresh powder."

"I wish I was dreaming about snowboarding too," I said, glancing down at the floor. The corner of the journal was sticking out from under the sofa bed. I kicked it with my foot until it was entirely out of sight. Then I stood. "Fine, but don't come searching for me when you're trapped in a horrifying nightmare!"

"You're hysterical, Zo," Matt said, snuggling down into his bed. "See you tomorrow." Just to be funny, he leaned over the mattress and stuck his face close to the floor. "Good night to you too, Scaremaster." He chuckled. "See you in my dreams."

Chapter Six

No amount of athletic training could have prepared me for skiing when I was this tired. I was in really good shape from soccer, and yet, after just a few hours of skiing, I needed a break.

Chloe was in beginner group ski lessons.

Matt had taken an hour snowboarding refresher class in the morning and was planning to explore the slopes on his own in the afternoon.

I'd signed up for an all-day ski lesson, but by noon, I was falling down so often, I was thinking that I needed a nap instead of another run.

I met Matt in the Snow Hut for lunch. It was a round building on the mountain, at the top of the ski lift. My group was going there, so I'd texted Matt what time to join us.

"Ditch the group," he said as I carried my tray with a burger and fries to a private table. "Let's go for a run together instead." He'd gotten a steak and potatoes for lunch.

I sank into a plastic chair and picked at a fry. "I'm so tired," I said, admitting defeat. "I might just want to go back to the cabin." I yawned. "I barely slept." Under my breath, I muttered, "Stupid Scaremaster."

"I slept fine," Matt said, taking off his helmet and hanging the straps on the back of his chair. He ran a hand through his hair to puff it up. "Like a rock."

"Bragger," I said, unclipping my boots so I could wiggle my toes.

Matt raised an eyebrow. "I can't wait for the rest of the Scaremaster's story!" He pulled his own lunch tray closer and picked up a knife. "If we're lucky, maybe tonight I'll have nightmares!"

"You don't want them," I said. "Not fun."

"I hope tonight *my* mom turns into a bat! She loves flying," Matt said with a laugh, making fun of my dream. "And when I go to the old lodge, I'll bring a coat."

I rolled my eyes. I regretted telling him the whole dream at breakfast. He'd been making fun of it ever since. To Matt, it was silly. To me, the woman in the velvet chair haunted my thoughts. I could hear her saying, "I am your mother," as if it were on repeat in my brain. It kept me up all night, and I could still hear the voice now if I let myself be still a moment.

Matt stuck the knife into his steak, then stopped. "Huh, that's weird," he said, looking down at the slab of meat. "Look, Zoe."

There were two strange holes in the middle of the steak. They almost looked like puncture marks. Around them the meat was brown, not the usual bloody red of a mostly rare steak.

"You're messing with me," I told Matt. "Nice try. Did a vampire suck the blood out of your steak?"

"Maybe," Matt said, thoughtfully poking at the meat with his fork. "And I am not messing with you." He raised his eyes and crossed his heart with his left hand.

"You're ridiculous. You can't make me have more bad dreams," I said. "I'm so tired, I am going to sleep like a log tonight no matter what the Scare-master writes." I rolled my eyes. "This feels like one of your tricks."

"It's not," Matt insisted. He flipped over the meat, and the same twin holes were on that side as well. They went all the way through.

I cast him a challenging gaze. "Prove it."

"I will." Matt picked up his plate. "Follow me."

The restaurant at the Snow Hut was a buffet with different areas for different meals. I left my burger on the table and followed Matt past the Mexican station to "Fine Dining," which was where the fancy steak meals were served.

There was no line for the steaks. Instead, a handwritten sign said "Closed." There were no servers or cooks at the station, and the cash register was covered in a thick white cloth.

"That's odd," Matt said, holding his plate in front of him. "It wasn't closed five minutes ago."

"I hear voices," I said, slipping behind the counter. There was a small kitchen in the back of the station area. "Let's find out what's going on." I gave Matt a small grin. "Wouldn't want you to get food poisoning from vampire steak."

"And I don't want to eat something that's ABC," Matt said. When I looked at him confused, he said, "Already been chewed."

"Right." I laughed. "Though I don't think vamps chew their food. It would be ABD."

"Eww." Matt stuck out his tongue. "Already been drank? That's just gross." He looked down at his bloodless steak and frowned.

We moved toward the back of the Fine Dining station, ready to walk into the kitchen, when suddenly Matt put out a hand to stop me. "Shhh." He froze and put a finger to his lips.

We ducked down below the kitchen window, where we could hear the chefs but not be seen.

A woman said, "I can't believe this is happening again! Such waste."

"Who would drain blood from the meat?" a man asked. "That's absurd."

"I bet it's the guys over at the pasta station. They're so competitive," the woman replied. "And holiday bonuses are being given out next week. They're trying to ruin our best customer service record."

I looked at Matt and whispered, "Strange."

He nodded.

The woman went on, "Mr. Wampir isn't going to like that we closed early today."

"Let's tell him it was a refrigeration issue," the man suggested. "Remember what happened last time we showed him the spoiled meat?"

"Ugh." The woman's voice cracked. "Bad memories. I thought we were going to be fired."

"He ran off shouting about how he was going to 'kill that woman once and for all!'" The man was getting closer to where Matt and I were hiding. We ducked lower beneath the window. "He's a little batty at times."

"He's just old," the female chef argued. "He cares so much about the lodge."

"He should retire," the male chef said, his footsteps clicking against the tile floor. He gave a small snicker. "Some people say he'll live forever....I mean he's been here since the begin—" The footsteps stopped. "Hey!" We hadn't noticed, but he'd come around the corner and was now standing above me and Matt. "What are you doing here?"

The male chef was short, wide, and bald. He looked like a character in one of Chloe's comic books. The woman he'd been talking to came out of the kitchen as well. She was tall and thin and had red hair. They were opposites in appearance and yet both really mad.

"You aren't allowed back here," the woman told us. "Kitchen's closed!"

Matt quickly held up his plate. "The meat is weird," he said in his most grown-up-sounding voice. I silently cheered him for his quick thinking. What better way to distract them from our spying than to complain about the food?

The woman and the man exchanged unreadable glances. She grabbed the plate from him. "Fine," she said, dumping the steak into the nearest trash. "Go get a slice of pizza. Tell the cashier that Janet said to refund the steak and that the pizza is on the house."

"Thanks," Matt said. We started to go around to the front of the counter, away from the kitchen.

"Oh," the male chef came close to us. In a whispered voice, he said, "Whatever you might have heard, forget all about it. I mean it. More than jobs are at stake."

"Okay, no problem," I said quickly, and Matt nodded. The man seemed satisfied, so we hurried away.

Matt got a piece of pizza, and we went back to

our table, where I'd left my burger. It was cold, but I ate it anyway.

The whole encounter at the restaurant was weighing heavily on me as I munched on my lukewarm fries.

"Matt?" I said at last. "I think—"

"I was thinking," Matt interrupted. "We need to go to the old lodge. I mean, why are we *reading* scary stories, when we could explore a real haunted house instead?" Matt swallowed his last bite of pizza. "I also think we need to find Mr. Wampir. The guy must be a hundred years old! I bet he has some great stories to tell!"

"Older than a hundred…" I'd considered that when the chefs talked about him. There was a part of me that hoped they weren't talking about Count Frederic Wampir from the Scaremaster's story, but rather his son or cousin or nephew. *Please,* I thought, *let there be a younger Mr. Wampir.* Because there was only one way that Count Frederic could still be alive…he'd have to be a vampire. That would explain the blood-drained steaks as well as the movement in the window of the old lodge. And the bats in my dream.

And it would mean that the Scaremaster's story was fact, not fiction.

"Want to go explore right now?" Matt asked me. Behind me, my group was getting dressed again to finish the lessons. My instructor called my name.

"I think I'll ski," I said, picking up my gloves and helmet. I was wiped out and skiing sounded terrible, but I wasn't ready to tell Matt that I didn't want to go to the old lodge with him. That dream had me spooked. He'd say I was a chicken, and he'd be right. Maybe I'd get my guts back after a good night's sleep, but in this moment—I wasn't sure.

"My parents paid for the lesson." I dumped the trash from my lunch tray into a garbage bin. "I'd feel bad ditching."

"Let's go tonight, then," Matt said, following me toward the exit. "After dinner."

"I hear there's a campfire," I said, rubbing my belly. "S'mores and cocoa...yum."

"After that?" Matt asked, glaring at me through his lowered yellow goggles.

I shrugged. "Maybe. I might be too tired." I hurried off to meet my ski group.

Over my shoulder, I could feel Matt's eyes on my back. I'd never run away from a fright before.

Never. Usually I sought them out. But there was a warning inside me that was telling me to stay away from the old lodge.

The Scaremaster and his story had done what no book or movie had ever done before—I was honestly afraid.

Chapter Seven

"I can't believe they left us to babysit!" I complained to Matt, though deep inside I was glad. Babysitting Chloe meant we could not go explore the old lodge.

I was acting incredibly lame, and I knew it. There was no excuse for me not wanting to go. Scaring each other was what Matt and I loved most. But there was something about that book that had set me on edge. I didn't want to read another story, or explore the lodge. Not tonight, anyway.

When Matt asked Chloe, "Hey, want to hear a scary story?" I was so wound up, I jumped out of my chair at the table and shouted at him, "No. She doesn't want to hear a story!"

It was embarrassing. I was out of control. "Sorry," I told Matt, forcing myself to sit back down and pick up the dice. It was my turn in

Monopoly. "That dream thing and then the meat thing—it's giving me a headache."

Chloe was on my side. "Zoe had bad dreams last night. They were so bad, she even left the light on to sleep." She smiled as if she was the more mature one. "I made her turn it off." She looked at me as if I was pathetic. Which was exactly how I felt.

"Mom said no scary stories," she told Matt. "But Zoe never listens."

This was getting worse. I rolled the dice and took my turn, then handed them to Chloe. "Go," I said. "You're close to owning another hotel."

"If you're lucky, it'll be haunted," Matt joked, but I didn't think it was funny.

Chloe shook the dice in her hands but didn't roll. Instead, she set them on the table. "I don't want to play anymore." Pushing back from the table, she said, "I want to have a dance party."

It was one of those things I did with her when Mom and Dad were away. We could never agree on something to watch on TV, so I'd come up with a few things to keep Chloe entertained while I baby-sat. A dance party was her favorite.

We'd change into fancy clothes, then turn the music up and the lights down. Sometimes, if I had time, I'd put up streamers and blow up balloons while she put on her dress and brushed her hair.

The dance parties were always fun. But now that she was mentioning them in front of Matt, I was self-conscious. My cheeks flushed. It all felt so immature and silly. I'd rather go to the haunted lodge than have a dance party with him.

"I brought a dress in case we had a dance party," Chloe told me. She twirled around in her jeans and T-shirt. "I can go put it on."

I didn't have anything that was dance-party-worthy. And besides, I was already in pj's. I'd put my fuzzy flannel top and bottoms on after my shower. They were new and had blue snowflakes printed on the soft pink fabric.

I clicked my tongue. "I don't have anything to wear," I told my sister. "Sorry." Behind me, I heard Matt snort. There was no doubt that he was on the verge of laughter. I'd never hear the end of this. He was definitely going to make fun of me for a long, long time.

"Maybe we can have a dance party another

night?" Chloe suggested. "You can borrow some-thing to wear from Mom!"

"Okay," I told her, hoping to end the subject.

"I have another idea." Grabbing my hand, she said, "I want to make snow angels." Chloe stopped me before I could protest. "You promised Mom."

I started to remind her that I'd also said we shouldn't do them in the dark, but Matt interrupted.

"Sounds fun," Matt jumped in. "More fun than dancing anyway." He grabbed his coat from the rack and tossed me mine. "We'll do it right outside the door."

I glanced down at my pajamas. "Really? How about you take her? I'll stay here."

"You have to come, Zoe. You promised!" Chloe eagerly scampered to the bedroom to get her gloves.

While she was gone, Matt said, "Let's run around outside, throw snowballs, make angels, and get her tired. Then, after she's asleep, we can read the Scaremaster's book some more."

"Sure." I gave up. Matt wasn't going to stop nagging at me until I agreed to either read the book or sneak over to the lodge. So with those as my options, I decided that reading the book was better than exploring the lodge. Plus, I was so tired I wasn't going to have bad dreams, no matter what the story said. I knew I was going to sleep like the dead.

"Fine," I said with a sigh. "Let's make angels. Where's my scarf?"

I tucked the bottom of my pajamas into my boots, slipped on my ski pants, put on my coat, and covered all my skin. Chloe was all covered up too.

Matt was willing to brave the cold. He had his coat on but no ski pants.

"I'm not scared to get cold and wet," he said, as if that was a challenge to me.

I ran a hand over my ski pants. "This has nothing to do with fear. It has to do with brains, which I have. And you don't."

"Zoe!" Matt gave me a shocked look. "How could you reveal my secret like that?" He turned to Chloe. "Don't tell anyone. It's because a zombie ate my brains."

Chloe was into the joke. She screamed playfully and dashed out the cabin door.

It was bitterly cold outside but not snowing. We stayed in the light of the cabin windows and had a short snowball fight. Even though I was wearing my gloves, my fingers felt cold. We let Chloe hit us both with snowballs a few times, and then Matt knocked me down into a snow bank.

"That's for yesterday," he told me. "When you hit me with a snowball at the lodge."

"Now I'll need my revenge," I said, standing and dusting myself off. "You better watch out!"

He laughed, and I swore I heard his laughter echo.

That's odd, I said to myself. I shook off a feeling that we were being watched and told Chloe, "How about those snow angels?" My ski pants were already wet, so I just flopped down into a flat area right near I was standing.

Chloe lay down beside me.

Matt was hovering above us. His shadow blocked the moonlight.

"Are you scared to get your jeans wet?" I asked him. "Lie down already."

"I'm not afraid of anything," he told me with a chuckle, which again seemed to echo.

He settled next to Chloe and leaned back into some fresh powder.

"Snow angels, go!" Chloe announced, raising

her hands above her head and pressing them back into the snow.

This time, it was Chloe's voice that seemed to echo in the night. Like "Sn-oh-oh-oh…"

I raised my arms, about to start my own angel, when I looked up to the sky.

"Augh!" I screamed.

"What?" Chloe said. "If you're trying to scare me, it's not funny!" She stood up from her angel in a huff.

"Yeah," Matt repeated in her same tone. "It's not funny."

"Hey, Chloe," I told my sister. My words were tumbling out fast. "I screamed because snow got in my pants."

She giggled, just as I'd expected her to.

"Can you grab me a towel?" She was already standing, so I thought she might be willing. I added, "If you do, I'll make us some hot chocolate."

"With mini marshmallows?" she asked.

"As many as you want," I said, sitting in the snow and pointing toward the house. "Just get any towel, okay?"

"Oh, fine." With a big huff, she said, "Be right back. Don't mess up my angel."

"My tushie is too cold to move," I assured her.

When the cabin door shut behind her, I told Matt, "It wasn't snow that made me scream. Look!"

I pointed to the sky. It was a bat. It was circling our heads and zooming back and forth through the trees.

"Is that your mom?" Matt turned to the side to look at me. He was still lying in the snow. "Mrs. Lancaster? Is that you?" he called.

"Don't make fun of me!" I threw a handful of snow at him. It fell like a fine dust into his hair.

"Mellow out. We're in the mountains. Bats live in the mountains. What's your issue?" Matt sat up and looked back at the snow. "My angel looks like a snow robot. I forgot to move my arms."

Clearly, Matt wasn't making the same connections that I was making. "It's a bat," I told him. "Like Mr. Wampir's mother in the story."

He shrugged. "How can you know that?"

"I just do!" I replied. I couldn't explain it, but I just knew that it was like the same vampirish bat in my dream.

"At least it's not your mother," Matt said, smirking at me.

I stood up. "You don't find this even a little

scary? There are too many coincidences," I told him. "The music, my dreams, the meat...I think Mr. Wampir got turned into a vampire by his creepy vampire mom."

"That was all in the Scaremaster's story." Matt shrugged again. "It's a story, Zoe. A st-o-ry." He said that last bit as if slowing down his words would make me realize how insane I was acting.

"But it's coming true," I told him, my voice rising. "Things in the story are actually happening."

"Your imagination is running wild, Zo," Matt said, heading into the cabin. "You're too tired. Let's go in. You sleep. I'll hang out with Chloe till our parents get back."

The bat above my head squeaked in a long, high sound that hurt my ears.

"Your mom's calling," Matt said with a laugh. "Come on, sleepyhead." He opened the cabin door and waited for me to enter.

"Okay," I said, not quite convinced he was right. "Maybe I am too tired. We can start fresh with vacation scares tomorrow."

I went to find out what was taking Chloe so long with the towel. She'd never come back outside. "Chloe?" I peeked into the bathroom we shared. She wasn't there.

"Chloe?" I looked in Mom and Dad's room. "We aren't playing hide-and-seek. Come out."

She didn't answer.

My heart was starting to beat a little faster as I went room to room calling her name. "Chloe?"

"What's up?" Matt asked. He'd been in his parents' bathroom changing into dry pants.

"Did you see Chloe?" I asked him. I could now barely hear my own voice over the beating of my heart.

"Um, no, she wasn't in the bathroom with me—"

I smacked him hard on the arm. "No messing around," I said, my voice tight and my face flushed. "She's missing."

"No way," Matt said, looking around the living room. "She just came inside a minute ago. She's got to be here."

"She's not," I said. Just to be sure, I called her name one more time. "CHLOE!"

When we came in, we'd left the cabin door open. I could hear the bat outside squeaking, as if it were talking to me. I rushed to the door and peeked outside. The bat circled the cabin one last time, then flew off toward the old lodge.

"Matt," I told him, shaking with fear like never before. "I don't know where she is."

"She left a clue," Matt said in a voice so low I had to ask him to repeat what he'd said.

"What?"

"I know where she is." Matt held a creamy-white square of paper in his hand. "Our game was moved to the side, and the Scaremaster's journal was sitting in the center of the table." He pointed back toward his bed. "I made the bed into a couch this morning and put the book underneath a cushion. I swear, Zoe."

Goose bumps broke out along my spine and traveled all the way to my toes.

"The book moves on its own," I said. "It did that last night too." I put a hand on the cover. "Chloe would never read a story from this," I said, feeling a tingling warmth radiate from the pages. "She doesn't like to be scared."

"Maybe, but look at this." Matt handed me the paper he was holding. It was an envelope. "This was sitting on top of the book."

On the front on the envelope was Chloe's name in powdery gold lettering.

Inside, the card had an embossed golden W with two small red dots over the letter, at the top of the paper.

The invitation read:

Please join me this evening for a special celebration.

The final night of the Wampir Ski Resort and Lodge

Dinner will be served at 8:00 p.m.

Dancing to follow

"It's a dance party," I moaned as my legs threated to collapse under me.

Matt slipped a chair behind me, and I sat.

"A dance party," I muttered again. "Chloe went to a dance party." Gathering my strength, I rushed to the bedroom. "Her party dress is missing!" I shouted to Matt. "And her nice shoes." I came back to the living room. "And her coat and gloves. She must have gone out the sliding glass door and around the cabin so we didn't see her."

Matt looked at me. He was standing at the table, over the Scaremaster's journal. The book was open. "There's a new story," he said.

It began:

Once upon a time, there was a girl named Chloe.

Chloe loved to dance.

Chapter Eight

I dressed quickly in jeans and a sweater. Wearing my ski jacket and warm boots, I rushed outside with Matt. I was carrying the Scaremaster's journal and the two other invitations that we'd found tucked inside its pages. There was one with my name on it and one for Matt.

Matt had a backpack with the supplies he thought we might need, specifically, a flashlight and garlic. Well, it was actually garlic spread for the garlic bread that my dad had made us for dinner, but we figured it would have to do.

"I heard that a silver chain is good for fighting vampires," Matt said, zipping up his backpack. "Vampires can't break silver, so maybe we could tie up his hands?"

"If Mr. Wampir really is a vampire, I'm not planning to get close enough to him to tie his hands. And if his mom lives there too, we'd need two chains." I didn't even have one. "I think we are stuck with garlic spread and our wits."

"A stake?" Matt suggested. We'd left the cabin, locked the door, and left a note on the table for our parents saying that we had gone to see a movie at the lodge. I hated lying, but it was better than the truth:

Chloe has been abducted by
vampires.

Home by 10.

Love, Zoe and Matt

"Do you mean stake, as in a sharp stick to plunge through a vampire's heart? Or a steak, like at lunch? Just in case the vampire is thirsty for blood."

Matt shrugged and wrinkled his nose. "Both?"

I could tell he was trying to crack jokes to keep me from worrying too much. But I was worried. And he was too.

I looked around. There was so much snow on the ground that I didn't even see a stick. Again, I was not planning to get close enough to a vampire to plunge a stake through his or her heart tonight.

I was also scared. Really, really scared.

Matt grew quiet as we hurried toward the old lodge.

He put a hand out to stop me as we neared the front steps. "Read the story, Zo," he told me, pulling out the flashlight. "If the Scaremaster's stories are coming true, we need to be prepared for what's going to happen next."

That made sense. I opened the book and held it in the beam from Matt's flashlight.

Chloe loved parties. When the bellman brought her the invitation, she immediately changed for the dance. He assured her that she'd have a fun time. He said that Zoe and Matt would be there soon. Chloe agreed to go, and together they hurried out the cabin's back door.

The beam of the light flickered, and I tapped the flashlight impatiently.

I read on:

Tonight was going to be the most lavish party Frederic Wampir had ever held. It would make up for the disaster at the grand opening event all those years ago.

The tables were set with the finest china. The crystal glasses sparkled in the glow from the chandeliers. The band had been practicing for weeks.

This night would be one that no one would ever forget.

It was the last time a party would ever be held at his Wampir Ski Resort and Lodge.

I raised my eyes from the page. "That's it," I said. But as I said it, I glanced down to find that more words were slowly appearing at the bottom of the page.

To be continued...

I flipped to the next journal page. It was blank. "I don't know what it means," I told Matt. "What happens next?"

Matt bit his bottom lip. "We're going to have to go inside and find out," he said.

He started to move, but I held back. "Are you scared?" I asked. "Because I am. I admit it." I felt tears brimming in my eyes. "What if we can't find Chloe? Or what if she's already a vampire? What will we do?"

Matt considered my face for a long moment, then switched off his flashlight. "Don't stress yet," he said at last. "We'll find Chloe, and she'll be fine. Just keep repeating that, okay?"

I nodded. "I'll try."

He put a hand on my back as we walked together. "I'll let you know if I get scared, okay?" he said. "Right now, I have that bubbling feeling of anticipation. Like when you're about to enter a haunted house. Like when you know that things are going to pop out and try to scare you." He turned to me and smiled. "I like that feeling. It makes me brave. I'm going to use that bravery to find your sister!"

Channeling every drop of courage I had left in my tired body, I tucked the Scaremaster's journal under my arm. "Let's go," I said, stepping up over a broken board on the old lodge's porch and entering the lobby.

The lobby was exactly like I'd dreamt. Only now, there was one huge difference. It looked brand-new. The wooden steps of the staircase gleamed with polish. Brass rails that I hadn't noticed before glimmered under the light of a giant crystal chandelier. The paintings on the wall were all straight, not damaged, and there were no spiderwebs in sight.

I gasped. "Matt," I said, taking a steady breath. "What is going on?"

"Velcome to Vampir," a voice said from behind us.

I swiveled on my boot so fast that I nearly knocked Matt down as I turned. It was the bellman from the new lodge. The one who'd welcomed us before. He was wearing the same jacket and hat. I realized then that the uniform was timeless. It could have been from another era or from today. It was just a coat and hat.

"You!" I pointed at him.

The bellman gave me a curious look that revealed nothing. "You are here for the party, no?" He put out his hand to take my jacket.

"It's cold," I said, still sounding rude. "I'd rather keep it." I wrapped my arms around myself, as if my coat was some kind of protective shield.

Matt, on the other hand, gave his coat to the bellman. "I think it's warm," he said, taking the claim check from the man. He leaned into me and said, "I'm curious where he'll take it. To the coatroom from the past or the one from the present?"

"I don't know." This was all overwhelming. I couldn't tell what was real and what wasn't anymore.

"Your table is ready," the bellman told us, waving his hand toward the old ballroom. The doors were now fixed, or else it was all a ghostly mirage.

When we entered the grand ballroom, it was exactly as the Scaremaster's story had described, which was also the same as in my dream.

Beautiful tables set with fine china. A band

on a long stage played songs that I assumed were the same ones that Chloe had heard at the new lodge. They were certainly the tunes that I'd dreamt about.

The room was crowded with guests. They seemed too solid to be ghosts. Where had they come from? Their clothing was old-fashioned. Their skin was oddly pale. They didn't seem to notice Matt and me in our modern clothes, or if they did, they were too polite to stare.

I was struck by how many people were there, and yet, there had been no footprints in the snow around the lodge. I told myself it must have been too dark to notice.

"Have you seen my sister?" I asked the bell-man. I kept my voice calm and kind. I had decided that being rude wasn't going to help us.

"Mistress Lancaster is somewhere else," he said mysteriously. He pulled out a chair for me to sit. "Dinner will be served promptly."

I sat down, but the instant the bellman walked away, I stood.

"Matt, what are we going to do?"

"This is amazing," Matt breathed as he looked around. "This must be what the actual grand opening looked like. It's as if we stepped back in time."

"Right before the guests started disappearing and Wampir's mother showed up," I said. I put a hand on his arm and shook it. "Matt! We gotta find Chloe and get out of here."

Matt looked at the strange scene in the room. "I know—I'm sorry. I just can't believe what I am seeing is real," he said.

"Me either," I told him. "I think we're trapped inside the Scaremaster's story." I set the Scaremaster's book on the table.

"Let's see if he's written anything else," Matt said. He opened the book and turned a few pages. Then he read:

*Chloe was early for the party.
Mr. Wampir offered to take her
on a tour of the lodge before the
other guests arrived. She was
eager to go.*

*He put a hand on the back of her
neck and led her up the steps.*

"Neck! It says neck! That's a vampire's favorite place to drink from!" Matt gave me a look. I was shouting. "Oh." I glanced up at the people in the room. Oddly, no one turned to look at me. The music must have been louder than my outburst.

"Upstairs." Matt was out of the ballroom so fast I had to run to catch him.

"Wait," I said. "Was there more story?"

He stopped at the bottom of the steps and showed me the journal.

To be continued...

Chapter Nine

The instant we stepped onto the first step, a cold gust blasted through me. I blinked against the frozen wind, putting my hands into my pockets. My eyes watered, and my nose started running.

"Zoe." Matt tipped his head close to mine and whispered, "I'm not saying that I'm scared, but this is odd." He turned me slightly. I wiped the wetness from my eyes and could see that the stairs were now decayed. The banister no longer gleamed. And the pictures on the wall looked exactly like they had in my dream: torn, crooked, with cobwebs.

"What happened?" I asked him, wiping my eyes again to be sure what I was seeing was real.

"I don't know…." He stepped carefully onto the next step. It creaked under his weight.

I followed Matt as he climbed the stairs. He tested each board to check that it was secure enough to stand on.

At the top of the stairs, there were two ways to go. Both directions led to long hallways filled with guest room doors.

"We are *not* splitting up," I told Matt, grabbing his arm. "Don't even think about it."

"I considered it," he admitted. "But that never goes well in stories." After looking left, then right, he said, "We'll go left."

Desperate to find my sister fast, I yelled, "Chloe! Are you here?" I yelled it both directions. There was no answer.

"Okay." I sighed. "Let's start left."

We headed down the hallway. I was holding the Scaremaster's journal in my hand, when suddenly it felt warm.

"The Scaremaster has something to say," I told Matt. "Fingers crossed he's going to tell us where to find my sister."

Matt took the book from me and opened it. "There's nothing new," he reported after scanning a few pages with his flashlight. "We're at the same 'to be continued.'"

I looked over his shoulder. "Hang on, Matt," I said before he closed the cover. "Something is happening."

The tour began on the second floor. Room 18 was Chloe's favorite.

"Is that it?" I shouted to the book, as if it could hear me. "Come on, Scaremaster, give us more! Where is she?" This was frustrating, and I was worried that time was running out for my poor sister.

I wished we had put a pen in Matt's backpack. Maybe we could have written some questions in the book that the Scaremaster could answer.

"We're in the wrong hallway," Matt said, heading back toward the landing. "Room eighteen is to the right."

I was on his heels. We were at the room a few seconds later. The door was closed. The number "18" hung sideways, but the knob looked as though it had been recently polished.

My blood felt like it had been replaced by taffy. I could barely breathe. I put my face near the door and said, "Chloe?"

Silence.

"Stand back," Matt said. "I'm going to break down the door."

"Uh, Mr. Macho," I said, blocking his path,

"twist the knob first. If she's in there, let's not hurt her when we barge in."

Matt puffed out his chest. "I'm on a rescue mission." He reached past me and turned the knob. The door opened easily.

The hinges creaked.

"Chloe?" Matt called her name, leaning in slowly. He shined his flashlight around the room. From the hallway, we could see an empty bed with dirty, torn lace covers, a broken window, and carpet that was moldy from years of weather coming in through a shattered window.

"Chloe?" I called again, stepping into the room. It smelled like dust and rotten fruit.

She wasn't there. But Matt's flashlight and our voices spooked the bats that lived in the ceiling. They flew toward us in a flapping mob. They were stinky, a lot like a massive wet dog. I ran into the hallway and ducked, putting my hands over my head to protect myself.

But they didn't want to attack. Instead, the bat mob soared past me and up a staircase at the end of the long hallway toward the third floor of the lodge.

"Whew," I said when my heart settled and

I caught my breath. I looked around for Matt. "Matt?" I couldn't find him.

Getting up, I went back to room 18. That's where I found him, lying on the floor, like he was making a snow angel in the carpet. He was face-up. His hands high over his head. Eyes wide.

"Matt?" I was certain something was terribly wrong. "Matt! Are you alive?"

He blinked at me. "You win," he said in a small voice. "That was so, so, so scary." Matt moved slowly to stand. "Who knew? I was fine with one bat when it was way up in the sky. But more than one—" He shivered. "Ick. Bats creep me out."

"I got scared first," I reminded him.

"But I got more scared than you," Matt said.

We were in an upside-down universe where we were arguing over who was more chicken. And my sister was missing. Could this night get any stranger?

I led the way back into the hallway. The bats were gone. I picked up the Scaremaster's journal. In the rush of the bat attack, I'd dropped it.

"I'm starting to hate that book," Matt told me.

"I already hate it," I said. "But we need it to find Chloe." I leaned the book on my knee. Matt had to go back into room 18, where he'd dropped the flashlight.

When he came out, I gasped.

"Uh, Matt," I said cautiously. I now knew that he was terrified of bats. "You have a friend."

"Huh?" Matt turned his head, looking back into the hotel room. "I don't see anything."

When he looked back at me, I touched my hair and gritted my teeth in a half smile. I figured a joke might lessen his panic, so I waved at the fuzzy little sharp-toothed bat. "Hi, Mom."

"No!" Matt shrieked, swatting at his head as if his hair was on fire. "No! Get off me!" He grabbed the garlic spread out of his backpack and started waving the open jar at the bat.

The bat flew off his head and began to circle us both. It squeaked and chirped madly.

Matt dropped the garlic spread and covered his ears. "Go away." He waved his hand, swatting at it.

I laughed for the first time since we'd entered the lodge. I'd read in books how people could be so scared that they'd laugh hysterically, and for the first time, that made sense to me. "Now that I know your greatest fear, you'd really better watch your bat...." I chuckled harder. "I mean 'back'!"

Matt rolled his eyes and pointed at the book. He clearly didn't feel like laughing. "Let's find Chloe," he said. "Anything new in the story?"

I held the book in the light of his flashlight. There was nothing new. We waited, thinking that the story would show up as we waited like before. But after a few seconds, it was clear there was nothing else.

The bat was flapping wildly above us, and no matter how many times Matt tried to get it to leave, it wouldn't.

"I think it wants us to follow," I said, thinking about the bat in my dream. This was sort of the same. "I hope that's not Chloe. What if we're too late and Wampir already turned her into a...a..."

"I don't think so," Matt said, though I could tell he wasn't 100 percent sure. He gathered his nerves. "One bat, I can handle. Let's follow it."

In the glow of his flashlight, we followed the bat. At the end of the hall, the bat moved aside and soared back toward room 18, leaving us at the base of a narrow stairwell.

"Do you think this is how guests went to the third floor?" I asked Matt as we moved slowly up the steps. I didn't want to crash through a board if the stairs weren't stable.

At the top step, there was a closed door.

"Let me." I offered to open it, in case we were facing another bat attack.

Matt didn't argue. He stepped away and put his hands over his head. "I'm ready."

I flung open the door. It was dark on the other side. I couldn't see a thing. "No bats," I reported when nothing flapped at me. Stepping into the room, I kept my arms straight out so I wouldn't run into anything. "I wish there was light."

Suddenly, as if granting my wish, a fire burst up in the fireplace. I was so surprised that I jumped back, bumping into Matt.

The warmth of the fire immediately heated the room. And the glow allowed us to see where we were.

We were in a living room area with two old couches and several small antique coffee tables. The window was broken, which reminded me that this was probably the room where I'd seen movement that first afternoon when we stood in our own cabin and looked out to the old lodge.

"I think this is the Wampirs' private residence," Matt said, drawing my attention to a shadowed area at the back of the room. There were about a dozen tables there. They were stacked in several long rows.

"Wow, the Wampirs really love collecting tables," I said, taking a step toward the collection.

"They aren't tables," Matt told me, stumbling back with a horrified look on his face. I thought he might make a dash for the door.

"What are they..." I started, but then realized. "Oh, coffins," I choked out the word. Now I was ready to run too.

"Let's—" I was pretty sure that Matt was about to say, "Go!" but then one of those coffin lids began to creak open.

I reached out and took Matt's hand in mine. He squeezed my fingers.

We were so curious that we couldn't stop watching it. We should have run away, but it was like our legs were rooted to the floor and we couldn't even look away.

The lid creaked as it rose, then stopped against its hinges.

A body began to rise. The first thing I noticed was the white dress. It was frilly, like a wedding gown, but the body inside was small.

I dragged Matt backward. "Vampire!" I shrieked.

"Really?" a small voice came from the coffin. "No way! Where?" The vampire laughed.

"Huh?" I turned around to find Chloe sitting up in a shiny, polished black coffin that was just her size.

"Hi, Zoe!" my sister greeted me. Then to Matt she said, "Boo!"

Chapter Ten

"That's not what vampires say," Matt told Chloe, rushing to help her out of the coffin. "Come on, we have to get you out of here."

"What are you talking about?" Chloe asked him, climbing out of the coffin. She reached back in to get her jacket. She'd been using it as a pillow. "It's so comfy in there. Want to try one?" She pointed past her small coffin to some of the bigger ones. "I'm sure they have your size."

"Chloe, stop fooling around."

Once Chloe was out, Matt closed the coffin lid.

I rushed to my sister and hugged her so tight she said, "Can't breathe. Get off me!" Chloe shoved me back. I gave her a little space but didn't let go.

"I'm happy to see you." I checked her neck. "Did they bite you?" I was so relieved to find her. I didn't even care if she was a vampire. My vampire sister. It would be okay. We'd take her to a doctor, get her therapy, feed her bloody steak at every meal.

"What?" Chloe asked. She reached up to touch her own neck. "Of course not."

"We'd better hurry," Matt told me. "Whoever stuffed her in that coffin is going to be back soon."

"Is it time for the party?" Chloe asked us. "Mr. Wampir promised he'd dance with me."

"Of course he did," I said sarcastically. I'd let her out of the hug, but I was still holding her hand. "Let's go!" I carried the Scaremaster's book in my other hand.

We went down the narrow steps, through the hall toward the main staircase. Chloe tugged me to a stop at room 18.

"Wanna go in?" she asked with a mischievous glint in her eye.

"We've been there," I told her.

"Scary, right?" She smiled and then pulled her hand away from mine. "Squeak, squeak," she cried, flapping her hands and running in circles around me.

"Are you sure a vampire didn't bite you?" Matt asked her, looking baffled by her behavior.

"Are you sure zombies didn't really eat your

brains?" Chloe shot back. "You're acting so weird." She looked at me. "Both of you are nuts." She flapped around me one more time.

We reached the top of the large staircase. The lobby was still run-down. "Be careful," I told Chloe, who was jumping down two stairs at a time.

"When did you become such a scaredy-cat?" my sister asked me, landing on a creaky board with a bang.

"When did you become so brave?" I countered.

"Mr. Wampir told me there's nothing to be afraid of," she answered. Then, hearing music from the grand ballroom, she ran before I could stop her. "And I don't feel afraid anymore. Not of anything."

"Of course that's what Wampir told her," Matt said as he rushed to catch up. He spoke in the bellman's accent. "You von't be afraid when I turn you into a vampire...."

"We have to get her out of here!" I said, now realizing that the only one of us who wasn't afraid was my sister.

The party in the ballroom was more crowded than when we'd first come into the old lodge. There were people at the tables, enjoying dessert. And people on the dance floor, spinning to the strange music.

"Where is she?" I scanned the room.

"There." Matt found her first. Chloe was running around the room, excitedly checking everything out.

I'd never seen Chloe misbehave like this. She'd reach out toward waiters to touch trays of food, then pull back her hand without taking anything. But no one seemed to mind her there, even when she was poking at the dancers or cutting between couples.

When she saw me and Matt, Chloe ran back to us.

"We almost missed the party!" Chloe exclaimed. "I was tired from skiing and snow angels and wanted a rest, so Mr. Wampir let me stay upstairs for a nap. It was just supposed to be five minutes. I almost slept through the whole thing. I'm so glad you came to find me."

I cast a nervous glance at Matt. "Chloe, the thing is, Mom and Dad will be back from dinner soon. We need to go to the cabin."

"Just a few more minutes," she begged me. "I want you to meet Mr. Wampir."

"Where is he?" I asked, though I'd really prefer to leave right away. But something told me this wouldn't be over until we faced him.

"I'll find him," Chloe said, then dashed off into a crowded part of the room.

"Wait!"

She disappeared into a sea of dancing guests.

I didn't know what to do. The Scaremaster's journal felt strangely heavy in my hands. I gave it to Matt.

"I think he's ready to tell us more," I said, keeping an eye pinned to the spot where I saw Chloe disappear.

"I'll read it," Matt said, opening the book. "But I'm with you—this feels all wrong. We should go."

Where was Chloe?

Matt read from the journal. The first few sentences weren't anything we didn't know. They caught us up to now.

Matt and Zoe found Chloe on the third floor in the Wampirs' home. She was napping in a coffin exactly her size.

Chloe was happy to see them.
She wanted to go to the party.

When she entered the ballroom,
Chloe disappeared into the
crowd of ageless guests.

"Hmmm, ageless guests is an interesting way to describe them," Matt said.

"They do seem ageless," I replied. "Interesting." I again noticed that the dresses the women were wearing seemed from another time. The men were wearing coats and ties and hats that also looked pretty old-fashioned to me...but I certainly wasn't an expert.

"My bad feeling is getting worse." Matt raised his eyes from the page. "Do you see her?"

"No. What do you think is taking her so long?"

"Hang on," Matt said. "More words are appearing."

Matt took a heavy breath before continuing.

The scene was set, the same as
it had been more than a hundred

years ago. Mr. Wampir was outside, searching for his missing guests.

The band was playing "happy" tunes, and the waiters were serving dessert.

I stopped Matt there. "Oh! I should have remembered." I turned around just as the doors to the grand hall shut. I could hear them lock tight. "We're too late. We're trapped!"

"Should I break down the door?" Matt asked me.

"You're kidding, right?" I ran over to the doors to check. Sure enough, they were locked. I turned around and called, "Chloe!" but the music was too loud. She'd never hear me.

"I think we should keep reading," Matt said, pointing at the page.

I was scared. Matt was clearly scared too. This was the worst, scariest story ever!

I was about to run around and look for Chloe, but Matt started reading, so I stayed.

*The music suddenly changed.
Instead of the happy dance tunes
Count Frederic had requested,
the band was playing a slow
march with a steady rhythm
and clashing chords. It was a
Romanian song that he hadn't
heard in many, many years. Not
since the disastrous party, all
those years ago.*

"It's happening," I said as the music in the room changed.

Matt read the passage again and said, "If this is right, Mr. Wampir should be here."

"Yes!" I said, finding an older man, about my grandfather's age, walking into the room. He was wearing a tuxedo with long tails and a tall hat. With his short beard and brass-topped cane, he looked like he'd stepped out of my history book from school.

He was dancing with Chloe.

He turned her around so that he was facing me.

Our eyes met. And then Mr. Wampir raised his hand. He had Chloe's small palm tucked into his. The old man smiled. He seemed happy, and yet, there was something in that smile that set off a red flag.

"He wants to keep her!" I told Matt. "I swear that's what his facial expression means. He's never going to let Chloe go home."

"Calm down," Matt told me. "If what the Scaremaster says in his story comes true, then Chloe's not staying here. That's not in the story."

"Not yet," I protested. "We aren't at the end!" I was in a panic. Every nerve in my body was tingling and sweat broke out on my forehead. "I have to save my sister."

I took off across the room, running past dancers who didn't look at me as I bumped them or... wait. Why didn't they look at me? I forced myself to stumble forward, falling pretty hard on a man's toe. But the man didn't say a word. In fact, he just kept on dancing, moving away from me as he led his partner into a dip.

What was going on?

I was almost to Mr. Wampir when I slowed. I put my hand out toward a young couple dancing nearby and was shocked when I touched them and they didn't react.

"Bizarre," I said out loud, my fear temporarily replaced by confusion.

"Yes. Strange, but also amazing," Mr. Wampir responded to me, as if I'd spoken to him. He and Chloe stopped dancing. We all stood together in the middle of the dance floor. "They are holograms."

"I thought holograms were tricks of light," I told Mr. Wampir. "The dancers feel solid."

Mr. Wampir laughed, warm and friendly. "Isn't the modern world wonderful? They are created from ultrasonic waves that, when used with holographic projections, create something that can be touched. It's so incredible that all this is right at our fingertips. You saw the front hall was exactly as it was the day of the grand opening. The beauty of this room is created from visual effects. The band doesn't exist at all. And everyone you see is one of these new types of solid holograms." He smiled. "Except for you, Matt, Chloe, and, of course, me."

Chloe let go of Mr. Wampir's hand and moved to my side. I was glad he let her go and happy she was now within reach so that I could grab her for our escape. "Mr. Wampir is making a haunted house here at the old ski lodge." She grinned up at me and laughed. "It's gonna be the best! You were so scared!"

I turned to Matt, who'd just caught up in time to hear Mr. Wampir's explanation of everything we'd seen. "Have you ever seen anything like this?"

"No. Never." Matt shook his head. "I've been to tons of haunted houses. This one takes the prize."

Chloe stood proud. "Mr. Wampir told me it was all part of the haunted house and there was nothing to be afraid of. That made me brave."

My sister had danced with holograms in a haunted house. She'd been swarmed by bats, which I now thought might be some kind of furry drones. And she had napped in a coffin. We'd come a long way since she'd freaked out about Matt's body bag in the van on the way here.

"Thank you," I told Mr. Wampir. "Thank you for being so kind to Chloe." As strange as this all was, I meant it.

"He's trying the scary stuff out this week," Chloe said. "Only a few people were invited tonight. We're so lucky!"

I glanced around. There were no other non-hologram guests like us, so who else got invitations?

"Chloe, we gotta go." We had to get home before our parents. "Say good night, please."

"Before you go, would you like to see the grand finale for the ball?" Mr. Wampir asked us. His accent was very thick. I wondered how long he'd been in the country. He seemed younger than the chefs at the Snow Hut had led me to believe. He didn't look old enough to retire.

"Sure." Any fear that Matt had bottled up while we explored the old lodge was gone now that he knew it was all a setup for a haunted house. He was ready to be scared again.

"It's terrifying," Mr. Wampir said with a wink.

"You sure?" He looked to Chloe.

"I can handle it," she told him, giggling. Of course, she held my hand, crushing my fingers in a death grip.

"We're all set," I said. Then to Chloe, "One big scare and we have to go home. No nightmares, okay?"

"Promise," she told me.

"So here we go." Mr. Wampir moved away from us and raised his hands. "It is the final night of the old Wampir lodge. Tomorrow the building will be torn down so that a spa could be built for the new lodge."

It was quite a dramatic performance. I recalled how the invitation said this was the closing night. That was a nice touch. It added finality to the evening, as if we were the last ones who'd ever see the haunted house. I assumed every night of the "show" would be the "last."

"We've lived here for more than a hundred years," he said. The music faded, and the guests stopped dancing. Everyone was looking at Mr. Wampir.

Inside my jacket, my skin began to feel cold. I looked down to make sure Chloe's hand was still in mine.

She didn't seem scared at all. In fact, both she and Matt were smiling.

Mr. Wampir held up a black box with a large red button on it. He spoke to all his guests. "I've known each of you since the grand opening and have welcomed you into my family." There was a sadness in his voice. "Tonight we say farewell." He lowered a dark mask across his eyes, like the blackout ones some people use for sleeping.

The hologram guests looked at each other, side to side, with expressions of horror.

I had to admit, this was a very frightening show.

"*Unu. Doi. Trei,*" Mr. Wampir counted, in what must have been his native Romanian. On three, he pressed the button, and the chandelier above the room burst with a light as bright as the sun.

I had to look away, but before I did, I could see the holograms bursting around me. The men and women twinkled and then turned to dust.

The room faded back to the run-down, decayed space from my dreams, and a cold wind whispered through the cracked windows.

The chandelier's burst of light faded, and it took a minute for me to stop seeing spots in my eyes. Matt and Chloe were rubbing their eyes.

Mr. Wampir removed his eye mask and said softly, "This is how it ends."

Chloe began to clap. "That was so scary!" she told him. But there was an expression on Mr. Wampir's face that made me hold back from applauding. He was frowning, eyebrows drawn together. He looked miserable.

"Mother," he said, talking to someone behind us. "It's over."

Matt and I turned, and I knew then that the show hadn't ended.

A red velvet chair now sat on a raised platform at the back of the room.

That wasn't where the chair had been in my dream, but the chair itself was the same. And the woman, she was also the same. She was young, maybe thirty years old, with dark hair, wearing the same red dress I'd imagined. It had a high lace neck, and she was wearing long white gloves.

"It's over," Mr. Wampir said again, the sorrow causing his voice to crack.

She nodded and said, "It's time to move on, my child."

He didn't say anything; rather, he looked back at the piles of dust from the holograms that were now swirling around the dance floor as the wind picked up.

The woman looked to me and said, "Let us walk you out." She unlocked the large ballroom doors, which made me wonder what trick she'd used to get in there. Matt and Chloe were looking at each other like this was the best night of their lives.

The bellman stood at the broken, termite-eaten front door to the old lodge, holding Matt's coat. He handed Matt the jacket, and while Matt put it on, Mr. Wampir joined his mother on the front steps.

"Thank you again, Mr. Wampir," Chloe said, giving the man a final hug before we left.

"Yeah, thanks," Matt said, still smiling. "This really was the best haunted house I've ever seen."

I shook hands with Mr. Wampir, then went to shake hands with his mother. As she reached out, it crossed my mind to wonder how it was possible that Mr. Wampir was older than his mom. I passed it off as another clever trick for the haunted house. Of course, if they were playing at being vampires, it made sense. Vampires stop aging at the time they are bitten. So Mr. Wampir would be older, since the story said he'd run away from home. If he was the real Wampir, the woman must be an actress.

They'd paid so much attention to details: There was the whole Wampir play on the word "vampire." And the coffins. And the bats. And the blood from the Snow Hut steak, which I now imagined must have been used in another part of the haunted house. We hadn't seen it all. Plus, who knew— maybe the Scaremaster's book was all part of the setup too.

I had to admit, they'd done a terrific job. Maybe we could do another run-through before we left town?

I'd ask Matt and Chloe if they wanted to before we asked. I was certain they'd say yes.

I reached out to grasp Mrs. Wampir's hand in mine. It was cold and bony, and when I looked, the skin on her knuckles reflected that of an old woman.

We held hands in silence for a long moment, until she pulled back.

In an accent thicker than Mr. Wampir's and the bellman's combined, she said, "Gud-bye." Then, as we walked down the steps toward our cabin, she called out, "It vas nice to see you again, Zoe."

Chapter Eleven

We got home before our parents. Chloe was in bed when they arrived. We'd made her promise never to tell anyone about what happened tonight. From the way she agreed, I felt pretty sure that from now on, she'd be one of the best secret keepers in the world.

"How was your night?" Mom asked me as she, my dad, and Matt's parents entered the cabin and took off their boots and coats. We were sitting on the couch, flipping through some of Chloe's comic books.

"Boring," I said with a yawn.

"We were too tired to do much of anything." Matt leaned back into the couch. The Scaremaster's journal was hidden behind the cushion. "How was dinner?"

"Good," Matt's mom said. "We're also exhausted." She hung her coat on a hook by the door. "You two ready for another big day of skiing and snowboarding tomorrow?"

"Yes!" we said at the same time.

I was excited about skiing again, but first, I needed to sleep without nightmares.

"Hey, Mom," I started. "Would you mind if Matt and I ran over to the lodge? I read on the resort schedule that they are serving s'mores in the lobby tonight."

"Old lodge or new lodge?" Mom asked. As far as she knew, we hadn't gone to explore the old lodge yet.

"New, of course," I told her.

Mom consulted with the other parents, and they agreed. "You did a good job with Chloe. She's safe and sound in bed, so you can go. But just for an hour, okay?"

"Busy day tomorrow," my dad added. "I signed you up for another full-day lesson!"

"Oh, great," I said. I was going to guarantee that I'd enjoy it.

When our parents went to their rooms, Matt said, "I'm not hungry, are you?"

"S'mores was just an excuse," I told him. "We're going to return the Scaremaster's journal to the library."

Matt looked at me long and hard. "You don't want any more scary stories?"

I didn't even hesitate. "Nope." I added, "Though I'd be willing to take another trip to the haunted lodge, if you want."

"Cool," Matt said. "Maybe we can offer Mr. Wampir some suggestions to make it even scarier."

"I don't know what I'd add," I said, putting on my jacket. "It was scary enough. I'm actually relieved it was a setup for a haunted lodge attraction, and not a real haunted lodge."

"Real frights would have been awesome!" Matt said, getting his coat.

"You nearly died from the fake ones." I laughed. "Seriously, I thought you might have been scared to death when the bats attacked."

"I wasn't *really* scared," Matt protested. We were walking to the lodge now. "But you should have seen your face when Mrs. Wampir said, 'Gud-bye.'" He imitated the way she'd said it.

I'd almost forgotten about that. "I can't actually figure that part out," I told him. "She said, 'Nice to see you again, Zoe.'"

"That's when your face went pale," Matt

said. "I thought you were going to faint. What happened?"

"I'd seen her in my dream," I said, reminding him about the woman who had insisted *she* was my mother.

"You must have seen her somewhere else too." Matt opened the lodge door, and this time we went in without messing around. "Was she at dinner in the dining room? Or skiing the slopes?"

I shrugged. "I don't remember. I think only in my dream."

Matt turned the Scaremaster's book around in his hand and ran his fingers over the leather. "Another mystery," he said. "But if everything else in the story can be explained, I'm sure there's a reason she recognized you."

It felt like a missing puzzle piece. "Let's just get rid of the book. Then we can go back to scaring each other."

"I like that," Matt said with an evil grin. "In fact, I already have some ideas."

We went into the lodge's lobby. There was a door on the library room. It was shut. I pulled the handle. "Locked," I reported.

"Was there a door there before?" Matt asked me.

I hadn't seen one, but I might have forgotten.

We headed to the front desk. The man at the counter was hunched over, sorting mail into piles. There was no one else around.

"Excuse me," I said. "Can you open the door to the library?"

Matt explained, "We borrowed a book and would like to put it back."

The man slowly set aside the mail and even more slowly turned toward us.

"Library?" he asked, pushing up his thick glasses to see us better. "There's no library at the lodge."

"Sure there is," Matt told him. He pointed at the locked door. "It's over there."

The man shook his head. He was the oldest man I had ever met. His back was hunched with age, and his eyes clouded. I was pretty sure he took those yellowed teeth out at night. He waved a wrinkled hand toward the library door.

"That's a storage room," he told us. "Do you need a broom?" He gave a little chuckle at his own joke.

I held up the Scaremaster's journal. "We need to put this back."

"I've lived at the lodge my whole life," the man said. "There's never been a library." He considered it for a long moment, then said, "It's a good idea. I should make one."

Matt moved in closer to the registration desk. "You say you've lived here your whole life?"

"My parents built this lodge," he said in a proud voice. "I'm Joseph Wampir."

"Are you related to Frederic Wampir?" I asked him.

The cloud in Joseph's eyes seemed to fade when he said, "How do you know about my Uncle Frederic?"

"We met him," I said.

"Impossible," he said flatly.

Things were starting to get weird again. A part of me wanted to throw the Scaremaster's book in the trash and run back to the cabin. The other part wanted to know what was going on.

"You didn't meet Freddy," Mr. Wampir told us. "That's ridiculous. He was dead before my parents came to the mountain. We came to take over the ski resort and build this lodge."

"Why didn't you use the old lodge?" Matt asked. It was one of the thousand questions now floating in my head.

Old Man Wampir shook his head and looked at us as if we'd come out of a spaceship. "You can read, right?"

"Of course," I reminded him. "We were looking for the library."

"Right." He shook his head, as if just remembering we'd said that.

He reached under the registration desk and brought out an old scrapbook. He blew dust off the cover. "This has photos and newspaper stories from the very beginning of the Wampir Resort and Lodge." He pushed the book toward us.

Matt reached forward and opened to the first page. There was a photo of the old lodge, looking beautiful and ready for business.

"Opening day," Mr. Wampir said. He pushed Matt's hand aside and turned to the next page. "Such a tragedy."

There was an article from a newspaper.

Disappearances Reported at Wampir Ski Resort and Lodge.

"A hundred people," Mr. Wampir said, running his finger down the newsprint. "Maybe more."

"A hundred people disappeared?" I said, my voice came out small and confused.

"The staff, the chefs, the musicians, and all the guests," he said, shaking his head and sighing heavily. "They'd gathered in the ballroom for an opening night dinner and dance party. They were never heard from again."

"Who wrote the article?" I asked, something from the Scaremaster's story was coming into my memory. "There was a reporter there with her husband, right?"

Old Man Wampir looked at me sideways. "How would you know that?"

"She heard a story," Matt put in quickly. He asked, "Is the reporter the one who wrote this article?"

"Yes." Mr. Wampir closed the scrapbook and set it back under the counter. "She'd gone outside for a breath of fresh air, and when she returned, all the doors were locked. By the time the police arrived at the lodge, the rooms were empty. The entire resort was empty. The reporter never saw her husband again."

"Does anyone know what happened?" I asked, hopeful that there was a reason.

"No," Mr. Wampir said. "My father was Count Frederic's brother. We came right away and closed the lodge. My father decided to start fresh and began construction on this new lodge. It's been recently renovated." He handed us a glossy brochure. The picture on the cover showed the resort as it was today.

"What about the old lodge?" I asked. "No one ever went in there again?"

"Not after that night. My father locked it tight and closed it to the public," he said. "I worry about the building. I have always been concerned that nosy kids"—he looked directly at us—"would go to explore the house and get hurt." He paused, then said, "Or scared." As if being scared was worse than getting hurt.

It sounded like he'd made the place completely off-limits. I considered that we'd been invited there, and that it had been really easy for us to get inside. Too easy, maybe?

Mr. Wampir went on. "Tomorrow morning the bulldozers are coming. The house is going to be taken down."

"But what about the haunted lodge attraction?" Matt asked. He was gripping the Scaremaster's book.

"Haunted lodge? That's ridiculous. We're a

four-star resort!" He seemed offended at the very idea. Mr. Wampir put another brochure on the counter. "We're creating the Wampir World Spa. Before long, we'll be a five-star resort," he added proudly.

"Spa," I echoed. I'd already known that was what was going on the site, because Frederic Wampir, or whomever we'd seen in the house, had announced that at the party.

It really was the last dance party at the old lodge. And we'd been there. When Frederic Wampir turned on the chandelier, I'd noticed it was as bright as the sun, and now I knew why. Sunlight killed vampires by turning them to dust. All those guests, the staff, the waiters, and even the band—they weren't really gone a hundred years ago. They'd been drained of their blood and trapped in the lodge. I knew from all the scary stories I'd read that they were called thralls. Thralls were slaves to their masters, blood-tied to the vampires.

They were gone now. I'd watched them all blow away.

Matt and I thanked Mr. Wampir and went to sit on that plush sofa where our adventure had begun.

"What are we going to do with this?" Matt set the Scaremaster's journal between us.

"Should we leave it here?" I suggested. The fire in the nearby fireplace crackled. "Maybe throw it in the fire? That would be the end of the story."

"No," Matt said, making sure the locking clasp was secure. "I have another idea."

Chapter Twelve

The next morning, we hit the slopes for a run before our lessons, but we didn't stop at the bottom of the mountain. We let our skis and snowboard carry us farther, toward the old lodge. Matt had the Scaremaster's journal under his jacket.

We dropped our equipment by a tree and walked to the front of the lodge. There was a construction fence around the building with clear signs that said "Keep Out" and "No Trespassing."

"Should we sneak in?" I asked Matt. We wandered the fence line looking for a gap.

At the far side, behind the building, there was a bulldozer riding over the snow toward the house. There was an opening for the machine in the fence. We went to it.

We stopped there and looked up at the house. It was just as creepy in the daylight as it was at night. I wondered what had taken old Mr. Wampir so long to tear it down. Maybe he knew his relatives roamed the halls? Then, with the puncture marks turning up in the meat, he realized that they were hungry and was worried that what had happened to the lodge's guests so long ago might happen again.

I told Matt my theory.

"Makes sense," he said. "Not sure what the Scaremaster has to do with it all, but let's get rid of the book and end this story." He raised the journal, like he was speaking out loud to the Scaremaster himself. "We're leaving your haunted book in this haunted lodge."

"Should we take one last look?" I asked Matt. I hadn't had any other bad dreams, so I was certain the story was over, but maybe we should check to be sure.

Matt opened the locking clasp and peeked inside.

There were four words in the center of the first page.

It said:

Scared you, didn't I?

"Yes," Matt admitted.
I agreed, "Yes, you did."

Then we shut the book and started walking toward the old lodge.

"Hey, kids," a man's voice shouted from inside the bulldozer. It was the driver. He was climbing out of the machine when he saw us. "You can't be here." He tapped a finger on his yellow hard hat. "Danger zone."

"We got lost," Matt said. "Sorry. We're leaving." Then to me he whispered, "Create a distraction."

"Oof." I pretended to twist my ankle. "Ouch!" I dropped to my knees.

"I warned you kids," the man said, coming toward me.

I moaned. Matt ran. He dashed past the construction worker, past the bulldozer, to a broken window at the back of the old lodge. I held my ankle and whined while he chucked that evil journal into the house, hopefully in the same spot where the bulldozer would make its first knock-down swipe at the building.

Matt hurried back, and I stood.

"All better." I leaned on my ankle as if testing it.

"Yes," Matt said with a grin. "It's all going to be better now."

We left the construction worker shaking his

head. I heard him mutter, "Kids..." Then I heard the engine of the bulldozer start.

I smiled. "That's enough scares for one vacation," I told Matt.

I got my skis, and Matt took his snowboard. We walked toward the chair lift. It was a gray day with snow falling and very little direct sunlight.

"It's not quite over yet," Matt said, pointing up to the sky. "I have one last scare for you, Zo."

Above us, three bats flew away from the lodge, soaring into the distance.

"There go Mr. Wampir and his mom," I said, waving to them.

"I'm pretty sure the bellman is the third bat," Matt said.

I nodded, and we stood together, watching them until they were out of sight.

"Come on, Zoe. Let's go," Matt said at last, turning to face the top of the mountain. "It's time to hit the slopes."

Epilogue

"Just five minutes, Mom." Nate Mullen checked his wristwatch. He was one of the few kids he knew who still wore an old-fashioned watch. Most kids just used their phones to check the time, but Nate loved wearing a real watch. "I want to check out this new book on *Ursus arctos*."

"Oh, I know that one!" Nate's best friend, Connor Fletcher, was in the backseat of the car. He leaned forward and said, "It's a kind of bird, right?"

Nate smiled to himself. "Yes," he told Connor. "It has sharp teeth and can fly backward."

"Wow, that sounds cool—" Connor started, then stopped himself. There was a long pause from the backseat before he said, "You're joking, aren't you? There's no bird that flies backward."

"Gotcha again!" Nate laughed. "You're an easy target."

Connor sighed heavily. "My brothers tell me that every day."

Nate was an only child, but Connor's family was big.

Connor was the youngest of four brothers. They all had the same dark skin, curly hair, and gray eyes. For a long time, his brothers had him convinced that his parents found him in the grocery store parking lot until Nate explained genetics to him. He looked too much like the rest of the Fletchers for the parking lot story to be true.

Nate's wavy red hair was also a dominant genetic trait. His dad was a brown-haired science geek. Nate got the geek from Dad and the hair from Mom. Though to be fair, his mom was really smart too.

"*Ursus arctos* is the scientific name for a brown bear," Nate explained. Then he asked his mom again, "Please?" He tapped the face of his watch. "We aren't supposed to meet our teacher for a whole half an hour. Can we go to the gift shop?" He clasped his hands together dramatically, adding, "Pretty please?"

Nate's mom was a librarian. It was hard for her

to turn down buying a book. Which, of course, Nate knew.

"Uh…" She was thinking about it as she pulled into a parking spot in front of the Natural History Museum.

"We can also get some candy to share with everyone at the sleepover," Connor suggested. "Maybe some gummy dinosaurs? We can identify them before we eat them."

"Oh, all right," Nate's mom gave in with a sigh and a grin.

Nate turned his head and gave Connor a wink. They were a good team. Educational gummy candy—that was a brilliant idea. How could his mom say no?

She handed Nate twenty dollars and said, "I'll bring in your duffel bags. Meet me by the ticket booth." His mom turned off the car engine. "Don't be late," she warned. "Mr. Steinberg was very clear about the time."

Nate nodded. Mr. Steinberg was their seventh-grade science teacher. He was young, funny, and the best science teacher Nate had ever had. He was also a big stickler for punctuality.

"We won't be late," Nate assured her, taking one last look at his watch. He and Connor got out of the car.

"Hurry," Nate told Connor. "Every second counts!" They took off running.

Two minutes later, they were inside the Natural History Museum gift shop.

Nate had been to a lot of museum stores, but this one was extra epic. The shelves were packed with all the kinds of stuff he liked. Rocks, minerals, puzzles, build-your-own dinosaur kits, boxes of fake bugs, dead butterfly dioramas, and books—lots and lots of books.

His head was spinning. If only he had more time. If only they could sleep in the gift shop instead of the museum!

Nate went straight to the bookshelf and easily found the book he wanted to buy. He'd seen it online when he'd looked up the museum and the exhibits. Nate liked to be prepared. He'd never been to this museum before, so he'd printed a map of the museum and studied the guides to the most popular exhibits.

The heavy volume had a big brown bear on the cover. Inside, there were "a thousand facts" about bears. Nate wondered how many of the thousand he knew already. He flipped through the pages. On page twelve, he found one thing he didn't know about bear habitats in Oregon. That small detail confirmed for him that he wanted the book.

"Connor?" he called his friend's name. They'd separated at the entrance of the shop. Connor went straight to the edible stuff, while Nate ran the other way.

"Over here," Connor shouted back. "You aren't going to believe what they have!"

Nate hurried around a display of T-shirts and tote bags. He wanted to stop and look at the shirts, but Connor was waiting. Besides, he didn't have enough money. The one book and some candy was all they could afford.

"Check it," Connor said, holding up a lollipop with a dead scorpion inside. "You're supposed to eat the bug!"

"Gross." Nate stuck out his tongue. "Yuck."

"My brothers would love these," Connor said. "Of course, they'd probably try to force me to eat the bugs for them...." He quickly put the suckers back on the shelf. "So, no thanks."

"Did you find gummy candy?" Nate asked,

looking over the shelves of chocolate "dinosaur eggs" and licorice ropes, with knot-tying instructions.

"Got them." Connor held up a big bag, which said there were five types of dinosaurs inside.

"The brontosauruses look especially delicious!" Nate said, taking the colorful bag. He added up the prices and realized there was going to be a little money leftover. "We have enough to get those licorice ropes too," he told Connor. "I want to try making the knots."

"Candy that comes with a book," Connor teased him. "You're predictable."

Nate laughed. They carried their choices to the counter, where an odd-looking woman stood at the cash register. There was no line, in fact, Nate noticed, they were the only two shoppers in the store. And yet, she didn't rush to help them. She didn't seem to be doing anything except standing there, staring at Nate and Connor.

The tall, thin woman had long black hair, pale skin, and a narrow nose. But that wasn't what made her odd. It was her eyes. When she first looked up at Nate, he would have sworn they were green, but a few seconds later, they seemed to be purple.

Nate glanced away and when he looked back, she was still staring, but now they were brown. They seemed to change color every few seconds.

Nate elbowed Connor to see if he was noticing the same thing, but Connor was busy reading the little pamphlet that came with the licorice ropes. He hadn't looked up at the woman at all.

"Did you know the strongest knot is called a Palomar?" Connor asked, pointing at an illustration.

"Those are best for fishing," Nate replied automatically, keeping his eyes pinned on the woman. Why hadn't she asked to help them yet? "A figure eight is best for climbing."

"Show-off." Connor shut the book and set it on the counter. "We better pay and get out of here."

"That's what I'm trying to do—" Nate whispered, again looking at the woman with the yellow eyes. "Um, excuse me?" he said loudly and in his most polite voice. "We need to check out."

"Oh," the woman said, as if seeing Nate standing there for the first time. "I see...." She reached out for their items and stopped. "You look very familiar," she said to Connor. "Do I know you? You look so much like the boy who..." her voice softened, and in a whisper, she finished, "disappeared."

"Uh, I've never been here before," Connor told her. He also shook his head. Nate noticed Connor's hands were shaking. "But my brother Chris told me about the kid who disappeared."

"Such a sad story," the woman said, gathering up the items on the counter and scanning them at the register. "A real tragedy."

"I thought Chris was kidding when he told me about that," Connor said. "It's not true, is it?"

"It's true," she said flatly. "Wait here. I'll be right back." She excused herself to get more museum store bags in the storage room.

The instant she was gone, Nate turned to Connor. "What story? What kid?"

"Chris was messing with me at dinner last night," Connor said quickly. "He told me that he knew someone who knew someone who knew the best friend of the sister of a kid our age who vanished from here."

"Vanished?" Nate echoed. "Like someone was kidnapped from the museum?"

"No. That's not what Chris said," Connor replied. "He told me that the exhibits in the museum are creepy, and that the stuffed dead animals in the displays come to life at night. The animals snagged some kid from his field trip. He was never seen again." Connor shuddered as a shiver ran through him. "You know, there are predators like grizzly bears and T. rexes and lions in the exhibits, so maybe they ate the kid. No one knows what happened. But he was gone in the morning and never seen again."

"Hmm," Nate said, considering the story.

Connor clearly did not want to believe it. He shut his eyes. "I told Chris it was bogus. I said he was lying." He opened his eyes again, wide this time. "But then a woman who works here says it's all true. Do you think it might be?"

Nate knew that Connor did not like scary stories. He hated scary movies. And refused to read scary stories. It would have been really easy for Chris and the other brothers to convince him not to come on the sleepover. One frightening tale about a missing kid, and Connor would have happily stayed home, safe in his bedroom.

"I'm sure it's a legend," Nate told Connor, putting a hand on his shoulder. "Your brothers are always messing with your head."

"That's what I thought too, until now." He pointed at the cashier. She was coming back their way with a box of store bags in one hand and a leather book in the other.

"But what if it's true?" Connor asked in a panicked voice. "I can't stay all night in a haunted museum! I just can't."

"It's not true," Nate assured him. "Displays only come to life in the movies. And if there was a kid who disappeared in the museum, don't you think the school would cancel all field trips and sleepovers?"

"I guess, you're right," Connor agreed, though he didn't seem convinced. "It's gotta be a prank." He looked at Nate and asked, "But how's it possible that the woman who runs the gift shop is in on my brother's hoax?"

Nate didn't want Connor to leave and go home. "It's a coincidence. This is a classic museum ghost story. Your brothers knew it because they all did the sleepover when they were in middle school. Now she's messing with us too." Nate was certain that was the truth. "I'll ask her. I'm sure she'll confess if she realizes how nervous this made you. Then we can all laugh about it."

The woman joined them at the counter. She took Nate's money and put their purchases in a bag. It wasn't until after she gave him the change that he realized he didn't see where she had put the leather journal she'd been carrying. At least, he assumed it was a journal. He hadn't gotten a very good look at it.

Before they left the store, Nate asked the woman, "Hey, about the missing-kid story. It's a legend, right? Like something everyone who works here says to make the sleepovers more interesting?"

She turned away from Nate and pinned her hazel eyes on Connor. "The story of Blake Turner is absolutely true. His spirit haunts the museum."

Read Nate and Connor's story
(if you dare) in

TALES FROM THE
SCAREMASTER™

HAUNTED
SLEEPOVER

SCHOOL OF FEAR

Sharpen your pencils and put on a brave face.
The School of Fear is waiting for YOU!
Will you banish your fears and graduate on time?

IT'S NEVER TOO LATE TO APPLY!

www.EnrollinSchoolofFear.com

 LITTLE, BROWN AND COMPANY
BOOKS FOR YOUNG READERS

Available wherever books are sold.

JOIN BEN AND PEARL ON A
WILD ADVENTURE
THAT'S ANYTHING *BUT*
IMAGINARY.

THE IMAGINARY VETERINARY SERIES
BY SUZANNE SELFORS

LITTLE, BROWN AND COMPANY
BOOKS FOR YOUNG READERS

lb-kids.com

BOB760

31901062541398

CPSIA information can be obtained
at www.ICGtesting.com
Printed in the USA
FSHW04n1923230318
46043FS

9 780316 464093